W9-BKF-092

THE MANHUNTER

THE MANHUNTER

LAURAN PAINE

OUTREACH SERVICES
Waterford Public Library
5168 State Center Drive
Waterford, MI 48329

Thorndike Press • Chivers Press
Thorndike, Maine USA   Bath, Avon, England

This Large Print edition is published by Thorndike Press, USA and by Chivers Press, England.

Published in 1995 in the U.S. by arrangement with Golden West Literary Agency.

Published in 1996 in the U.K. by arrangement with the author.

U.S.   Hardcover   0-7862-0397-8   (Western Series Edition)
U.K.   Hardcover   0-7451-2589-1   (Chivers Large Print)

Copyright © 1995 by Lauran Paine
Copyright © 1957 by Lauran Paine in the British Commonwealth

All rights reserved.

The text of this Large Print edition is unabridged.
Other aspects of the book may vary from the original edition.

Set in 16 pt. News Plantin.

Printed in Great Britain on permanent paper.

British Library Cataloguing in Publication Data available

Library of Congress Cataloging in Publication Data

Paine, Lauran.
    The manhunter / Lauran Paine.
      p.   cm.
    ISBN 0-7862-0397-8 (lg. print : hc)
    1. Large type books. I. Title.
  [PS3566.A34M28   1995]
  813'.54—dc20
                                                    94-45644

L. P.
Western

c.76 ten #175 $11.75 Middle

THE MANHUNTER

Chapter One

The supper fire glowed like a huge, congealed tear cast in bronze low against the earth, and the hush of purple night was thick with something Mark Carter could feel.

It wasn't the same thing that a woman would call intuition because men don't have it; they have restlessness of body and spirit instead. A worriesome effervescence that spirals outward from the pool of their awareness like the ripples in a pond when a rock is tossed into it.

Mark had it now, sitting cross-legged by the fire listening to the night. It didn't show in his face because the night was dark-engulfing, sweeping, with a vast core of silence to it, but it was strong in him nonetheless.

The fire showed below his face. Made him look like a bear wearing clothes. He was a big man — not tall, big. His neck was like oak, his shoulders sloped like a bear's shoulders sloped. His legs were great-thewed, his hands flat and broad. His hair was long and dull auburn and under some circumstances, like now, it glowed a rusty-red in a dark and curling way. He had lived over thirty years and it showed in the thrust of his jaw, in the unwavering hardness of his glance, in the lines of face and body. Experiences wrenched out of a life seldom mild gave Mark Carter a philosophy that fitted his hard, pensive look. As a lawman he had persevered; as a man who had been in almost every conceivable experience himself, he could think like the outlaws he hunted, could match iron with iron and courage with courage.

He kept his head in the shadows while he made a cigarette with lonely deliberation. A gust of wind ran its fingers through the dry grass around him, soughed off down-country and let the stillness, the silence, return. He lit the cigarette with something like worms crawling out along his nerve-ends. The restlessness stirred within him and he exhaled a squirting gust of smoke with his solemn dark eyes fixed and intent on the coals of his supper fire.

Exactly forty-five days trailing her. Forty-five days from the time he'd come back from San Saba and found the note. The trail hadn't been hard, the weather had held. To-morrow he'd ride down into Cascade and meet her. End of the trail.

He rolled carelessly in the rank-smelling saddle-blanket, clammy with horse-sweat, and his eyes, speculative, dark brown, wet-bright and as hard as sun-burst obsidian, lifted to the overhead where a ferment of heaven was splashed, slathered with thousands of flickering, moving lights.

The night was spring-balmy with the smell of earth rising up like steam around him. He ran a hand through his pressed-down hair, let the fingers stray down across his face. The skin felt slack-weary, sagging, to his touch. He was tired to the marrow of his bones. It had been a long trail, a long last day.

He thought again, for the hundredth time, of the note she had left him and pinched out the cigarette, relaxed against the earth with the odour of horse-sweat, salty, recognisable, around him. Drowsily his mind caught at the beauty he had ridden through this last day. Timber, sharp-etched hills with a yeasty iridescence to the sky that hung over all of it. Unlike the desert; a country with creeks in it, and shade. She had stopped at a good place. He fell asleep with the name of the town on his lips. Cascade. It blended in a musical way into his exhaustion, weaving a benign influence behind his eyes. Cascade . . . the sound of water tumbling over cool rocks — shade, trees, tree-sap in the air . . .

He slept on it and awoke with it still in his mind. He got up and stomped his sleep-swollen feet in his boots. The spurs gave off a musical ring. He smelt the clear mountain air, as bright and brittle as new glass. Softly jagged in the pearly dawn-distance were pine forests, a tinge of red bark against the deeper hues of sombreness. There was a definite, cool chill to the air as he went after his horses, led them up, saddled one and packed the other, ate a cold breakfast of left-overs standing up. Then he mounted and poked his way southward toward a strip of trees that stood watch on the lip of a drop-off, beyond which lay Cascade.

He breasted the rise, saw a shadowy town far off and rode down through a dark little arroyo that popped him out of its mouth like a seed. The sun panted its way up some distant sawteeth in the east and hung there, resting. Beyond the arroyo the land lifted sharply again. There were landswells and erosion gullies, yawning crevases deep enough to hide a man and a horse, and other vestiges of torrential rains that had come off the upland water-sheds in flash-flooding bygone years and bitten down hard and devastatingly into the shallow-earthed fringes of hardpan around the valley below. He rode on.

He reined up when the last frowning hillock broke away sharply under him and the valley lay exposed below. The village lay beside a strong, wide creek with scurling drifts of white-water in it. The buildings were old, unpainted, weathered to resemble the ground they stood upon. There were old trees, old when the first building had been built, and some wise, far-seeing hand had protected them. They made a shade that was pleasant, inviting, just to look at. There didn't seem to be much activity in the town. He lifted his reins and sought a downward trail, found one after passing through more trees and descended with the crinkled-cardboard hills in the far distance holding his attention.

He rode in expressionless silence his eyes probing the valley, the hills beyond, for signs of men or movement. It wasn't the reflex of a manhunter, that flitting study, that searching glance, it was the restlessness of a hurt spirit moving in human eyes.

Six weeks before, he had ridden out of San Saba with a wind-lashed roadway throwing spiteful handfuls of stinging grit into his face and his mind had never let him forget why he was riding even when he went through the towns picking up scraps of knowledge which enabled him to keep on. And always, behind his eyes, moved the pain that was totally foreign to what he afterwards did on the trail, instinctive things. Weeks and weeks of doing things he never clearly remembered afterwards, and now this; end of the trail. He knew she was down there, hadn't run any farther.

His shadow marched dutifully along on his west side as he edged toward the north-south road, and Cascade — its double row of buildings serene and peaceful, shady, spring-fragrant, already dozing in the water-blue of early morning — moved to meet him.

A few riders were abroad, a wagon creaked and groaned its way from the purple westerly distances and a buggy was led out of the liverybarn and tied in the shade of a crooked monarch of a live-oak.

The shadows of the mountains, of the swift-rolling traces of rich land slanted down hard upon the town. In their breath lay scents of pitch and spring flowers, grass. There was a plank bridge across the creek at both ends of town and before he got too low to see out and around, he knew there were other roads like filaments of a lazy spider's web, coming from any directions and ending in the fragrant dust of Cascade.

He shuffled through the dust of the road-way angling down toward the liverybarn. A man drifted out of the deep shadows of the runway and smiled at him. He swung down, stood wide-legged, solemn.

"You acquainted around here?"

The liveryman's smile grew broader. "Pretty well," he said. "I lived here all my life."

"Know a woman named Carter who lives here?"

"Carter? No, can't say that I do. New-comer?"

Mark nodded in silence.

"Well; I might not know her then. Folks come and go. The old families though, I know all of them."

Mark held out the reins and lead-rope. "Give them a wash-down and some grain, will you?"

"Be glad to. Stalled?"

"Yeah." He paid in advance and went out where the weight of heat smote him, moved along the plankwalk through intermittent patches of old shade toward the constable's office. A rider went by on a fast-walking bay horse, the pudding-dust muffling his hoof-falls. The door to the constable's office was half open. He ducked through it, met the calm, heavy-lidded stare of an older man

13

who was sitting in a chair rocked back against the wall gazing fixedly out through the open door.

"Howdy. Help you?"

A little streamer of wind brushed over the town, slid its belly over the roof of the constable's office and fled. Dust particles followed it.

"Do you know if a woman named Carter lives in Cascade? She'd have been here only a short while. A week maybe, not much longer I don't think."

The lidded eyes didn't move but Mark got the impression he was being measured and weighed by them. The chair came down off the wall with a sharp sound.

"Why are you looking for her?" The constable said it gently, routinely.

"She's my wife."

"Oh? And who are you?"

Mark fished out his old badge and held it in his palm so the other lawman could see it. The eyes flickered to it briefly then up to his face again. They seemed to be examining something else; they looked inward, withdrawn.

"I see. Well — yes, there's a Mrs. Carter come here about a week back."

"Where does she live?"

"You walk south toward the end of town,"

14

the slow, gentle voice said. "There's a cabin down there with geraniums . . ."

He went down there and knocked on the door. Gusty wisps of spring wind played with smoke that came out of a crooked stovepipe and beat against him in a fractious way. The dust made his eyes smart so he squinted them. He knocked again, just as a lull in the wind came, then she opened the door and they stood almost toe to toe, just staring.

"Can I come in?"

She stepped aside white-faced, silent, unbending. He closed the door and held his hat with both hands, looking at her. Something inside hurt him in a dull, persistent way. In his pain and anger while he tracked her to Cascade he'd thought of a dozen fierce things to say. Now not a one of them would come out; they didn't seem fitting.

"Why did you follow me?"

"Why?" He answered. "Because you couldn't — can't — just up and pull out like this."

She half turned from him, took several steps then swung back. "Can't? Mark, I have." She flagged off the words forming on his lips. "Don't . . . There's nothing to say. It's all old ground. It's all over and done with."

"Eileen, I — "

15

"I've heard it. Whatever you're going to say, I've heard it. I've heard it all." She jerked her head toward a closed door off the tiny parlour with its cut-out pictures pasted on the wall. "He's going to forget and I'll sacrifice anything to see that. He doesn't whittle guns all the time any more and tell everyone how his father is the best manhunter in Texas. He's going to grow up like a normal boy — the way he should have in the first place."

Mark stood by the door looking at her, feeling the abyss widening with each breath. Eileen at twenty-six was far more handsome, more desirable, then she'd been at sixteen. She was one of those women who blossom early and mature late. Youth lingered, would linger a lot longer.

"But why here? Eileen, if we couldn't have made it work, you didn't have to run away. I'd have given you money. It isn't fair to him, to you or me, to do it like this. Just run away."

"I wasn't trying to be fair," she said quickly. "I was trying to save a little boy from growing up like his father."

"There are worse things than lawmen."

"Are there? You've always said that. That's what I meant when I said I'd heard it all before. But, Mark, I'm not sure there's much difference between you and the men you hunt." She went over by the iron stove, turned and faced him. "Please, Mark — go."

"What are you going to do, Eileen? How'll you live? How'll Will get an education, a decent home-life? It's all wrong — this way."

She shook her head at him. "No, no, no! Mark, you're saying all the things I knew you'd say if you found us. All the things a man like you thinks."

"Well," he said, stung a little, "what's wrong with wondering how he'll grow up; what'll become of you?"

"Nothing Mark, except that those are secondary things to you. Manhunting is your first love."

"That's not true. I've told you a — "

"I know. You've told me everything you could think of and I know it all by heart, and it's all wrong. Mark, if we didn't have Will, didn't have a son at all, no children, what about me? Have you ever tried to imagine what a woman goes through every time her husband rides out after killers and outlaws? Have you any notion at all what that's like?"

She seemed to quiver without actually doing it. The room was warm enough, a little too warm in fact, and the scrabbling fingers of the spring-wind outside added to the drama inside the tarpaper shack.

"I don't want to talk about it any more, Mark, ever again. Never. I'm free of it, away from it, all of it, the killings, the manhunts, the fright you never knew about but that I lived with every day. I'm free of it and Will is. We'll stay free of it."

Very slowly he said, "Eileen, I won't let you do this."

"You can't stop me."

He stood a moment in silence then said, "Can I see Will?"

"He's not up yet."

"I won't waken him."

She led him to the little door off the parlour and opened it a crack. His son's dark hair was visible, tumbled and awry. His breathing beat slowly, regularly, under the quilts. Eileen reached in front of Mark and pulled the door to. They were close; so close he could smell the pine-scent of soap in her hair. As though she sensed his thoughts she turned swiftly and crossed the room to the stove, facing him across the room, large blue eyes bluer, full lips held in, arms crossed, the fingers gripping her flesh.

He went back to the door, stood there looking down. "I brought three hundred dollars with me," he said, and put it on a crate-table and raised his eyes to her face.

18

"Eileen, I don't want to fight you, to make you mad, to hurt you. Please don't make me do it."

"I won't, Mark. Just let me raise him my way. Like a normal boy."

"Without a father?" he said, letting his eyes lash the little room. "In a tarpaper shack? Is that normal?"

"It's the lesser of two evils," she answered. "I'd rather he lived like we're living now, in a tarpaper shack, than like we lived in San Saba with his father a notorious man-hunter and Will worshipping him, whittling wooden guns, practising drawing them . . ."

"Eileen, the banker's kid used to do the same things."

"I don't believe it."

He left her after that because they were talking in circles and he felt weary. Walked back up through the capricious little wind to the constable's office and went in there because it was second nature to be in a lawman's hangout.

Jonathon Buell, with his quizzical, steady blue eyes, had been making coffee. It smelled wonderful. He offered Mark Carter a cup and launched a conversation easily while they both drank. Mark's mind wasn't on the words at all until Buell fished around in a desk drawer and tossed an old six-gun without a

19

firing-pin, on top of his desk. He thumbed toward it and grinned.

"Your kid's gun."

Mark's dark eyes swung to the older face. "Whose kid?"

"Your's. Listen, Carter, Cascade may not be Chicago but don't peg all township lawmen idiots, either. The kid's a spitting image of you. He's told me all about you. Begged that old gun off me. Practices his draw in here by the hour."

Carter's gaze was like stone. "His mother doesn't know that," he said.

Buell shrugged. "I hardly know her. If Will don't tell her who would?" The blue eyes were thoughtful. "Wouldn't she want him playing with a gun? Shucks, that weapon's harmless."

"It's still a gun. She wouldn't want him doing that at all, anyway."

"Oh," Buell said, and he didn't sound surprised or chagrined at all. "Well; I can't hardly take back what I gave him or run him out of here now; can I?"

"I don't know." Mark sloshed his coffee, looking down into the cup where the grounds were. He fell into a long silence.

A big gust of wind rocked the building. Jonathon Buell poured himself another cupful; held up a graniteware pot and shook it at Carter. The big man stood up uncertainly.

"No thanks. I'd better be — "

"What's the hurry; you can't do much today. Weather's too bad." Buell crossed in front of Mark and filled his cup, put the pot back on the stove, went to his chair and dropped down in it. "How long you going to be around Cascade; any idea?"

"No, not exactly. Maybe — I just don't know."

"Well, say," Constable Buell said in that easy, friendly way of his, "while you're killing time how about riding up-country with me a little ways? A stage was held up there before dawn today. I went out and looked the ground over while you was down at your wife's place. The wind'll be bad but riding alone's worse; what say?"

Buell stood up looking across the desk into the larger man's troubled face. He tossed off the rest of his coffee. "You got a blanket behind your saddle haven't you?"

"Sure. Some tortillas too."

"Then let's go."

They rode out of Cascade with nothing more between them than that, but Jonathon Buell was the kind of a man who could do that, even with strangers. He was the kind of a man other men liked being with. A man could get to know him as well within a half an hour as he'd know him in a lifetime. A simple, straightforward man, one under whose layer of warmth lay an iron resolve, an undentable core of adamancy that never showed but which was there nevertheless.

Mark rode beside the constable until the road began to lift, both holding their silence. They broke through a shallow fretwork of trees, northwestward, and rode straight across open country where feed was stirrup high and ripening. Out of a clear sky Buell began to talk.

"A man in the law business up here," he said, "either gets his death of pneumonia or winds up with summer-fried brains. See that notch in the hills yonder? That's what they call Gunsight Notch. Used to be a wagonroad over it. All overgrown now. Just guessing, I'd say that's where they headed for, and if they did, that's the place they'll see us from. It'll take them most of the day to get up there. Good view from up there."

Mark roused himself and looked at the rugged heights then dropped his gaze to the land below the surge of hills. It was broken country with very little cover. "Be better," he said laconically, "if we could get some trees between us and the Notch."

"Pretty hard to do," Buell replied. Then, very suddenly he said, "Funny how people look at lawmen, isn't it?"

Mark shot him a glance and looked out over the sun-drenched range again. "Yeah; funny."

"Well; maybe that isn't the right word. Strange'd fit better. Anyway, folks don't like the law. Those fellers up ahead hate it. Mostly, folks realise the need for law but don't like it too much because it's authority and folks just plain don't like authority. Then there's other folks. They wouldn't live where there *isn't* any law but they don't like men who *are* law. That's the funniest — strangest — breed of all."

Mark's glance swung around slowly, thoughtfully, and lingered on Buell's features. His eyes, with the pain lurking in their depths, seemed quizzical.

Buell made an abrupt motion with his arm, westward. "Look there — what do you make of that?"

Mark looked. It was a dust cloud, straggled across the skyline like a dust-banner. Hung almost motionless in the crystal daylight. "I'd guess it to be Indians on the move. In Texas that's what it would be."

"Same thing out here. Poor devils. Know much about Indians, Carter?"

"A little," Mark said quietly, then, louder, more emphatically, "Enough to know if they run across those two holdups we'll be able to find out which way they went, get a description of them, their horses too."

"Maybe. Mostly, in this country, folks avoid Redskins. They aren't exactly hostile any more. They've had most of that stomped out of them, but the hate's still there, I know, and a single rider or a brace of riders could lose a mite of hair pretty easy if they didn't step aloft."

"What kind would they be?"

Buell squinted at the dust-banner as though it held a clue to the identity of the people making it. "Maybe Snakes — that's what we call Shoshonis hereabouts — or it might be Blackfeet. Hard to say. There're still some loose Sioux back up in there, too."

"Have any trouble with them?"

"Naw. Once in a while one'll go bravo or get skunk-drunk in town, but no trouble the way you mean it. Not in the last ten, fifteen years."

The direction of the Indians brought them closer to Mark and Jonathon Buell before they veered off following some ancient trail, broke over the farthest rib of land going eastward across the breaks, too far away for Buell to identify them. Mark watched them straggle past. He faintly heard the tumult of their passing; dogs barking, people yelling to one another, old squaws shrieking at laden horses and children adding their iota to the bedlam. It was a colourful, primitive mob of people who, since time out of mind, had been nomads in search of something and who were now seeking it all the harder.

Fortunately Mark and the constable were able to find the outlaw trail beyond the churned path of the Indians. Buell reined up gazing down at the ground.

"Looks like they split up here, Carter."

Mark hauled up and studied the ground. The imprints showed where two riders had milled. He had seen hundreds of trails like this one. He stood in his stirrups and twisted so he could see behind. The prairie lay like an immense carpet of new grass guarded by those huge purpled hills with their sugar-pine, reddish tinge. He dropped down and grunted. They'd crossed all that open country.

"I'd say they've seen us coming."

"That so? How's that?"

"Look behind you," Mark said. "If they stopped for a smoke or something before we got this far they'd have seen us." He looked down at the tracks again. "Why else would they stop here?"

"Indians," Buell said briefly.

Mark shook his head almost irritably. This was something he knew, this tracking men, knew it like the back of his hand. "How could they've seen the dust-cloud? The Indians were too far off for us to see them until just a little bit ago. Five miles or such a matter ahead, Indians wouldn't mean much to them. If they saw the dust from that far away they wouldn't worry about it. No — when they stopped here it was to study something. Since it wasn't the Indians, Buell, it had to be us."

Buell pulled at his scraggly moustache, craned his neck to look after the gaggle of Redskins far off on their right. His head followed the ragged serpentine a moment then he lifted his rein-hand and shot a final look at the forked trail.

Mark edged his horse away, quartering, seeking information from the ground. He finally drifted back down beside Jonathon Buell. "You know — they'd didn't really split up. I'll give you odds they did that to confuse us. Make *us* split up. The way they're riding they'd come back together up ahead somewhere. I'd bet on it."

Buell studied the younger face, then grinned. "Money?" he asked.

Mark's dark eyes warmed a little but his face didn't respond. "If they didn't do it they missed a good chance. Let's go see."

Buell poked along, still watching the distant

Indians now and then. Finally he said, "Maybe we could corral a straggler. They might know something."

"Let's just stick to tracks. Good thing it's spring not fall. I'm glad that little wind petered out." His mind pictured a humped-over rider quitting San Saba in the face of a grit-flinging wind. "I don't like wind," he said in a wintery way.

"I'm against rain, myself," Buell said conversationally, watching Mark's face with a close, shrewd look. "The first time I ever went after a man it was in the rain. Maybe that's why I don't like the stuff."

Mark said nothing. They kept on the trail until they hit a rising lilt of ground where scattered trees lay thick, fingering shadows athwart the trail. Garrulously, Jonathon Buell started speaking again.

"You mayn't like wind, Carter, but I don't think you dislike being a lawman. You're the type that makes a good one." He followed Mark, looking at the ground for a moment, then squirmed erect in his saddle. "Well — I didn't mean it just exactly like that either. I mean, you're the kind that makes a good lawman after you've acquired sense enough to go with the job."

Mark's dark glance lifted. "What do you mean by that?"

"Well — that's what I've been harping about since we left town. In a roundabout way, you understand. I've been trying to get the idea across that it takes more'n a fast gun and a star to make a lawman a good one. From the looks of you I'd say you've got the fast gun. Now, if I was to guess further I'd say you're the black-is-black and white-is-white type of sheriff."

"I was a deputy, not a sheriff," Mark said tartly, "and if there's some way to look at law-breakers that I don't know about, you tell me."

"Naw," Buell said. "I never learnt a whale of a lot from being told things, but I've never forgotten anything that got knocked into me. Besides, I'm wrong more oftener'n I'm right."

Buell shifted his weight in the saddle and dug deep in a pants pocket while the sun shone brassily off his russet face. He came up with a lint-encrusted plug of chewing tobacco. Worrying off a corner he eyed Mark apologetically. "Care for some? I don't blame you. Fact is — when I'm in town I don't use it either, but I got to sort of like the stuff years back when I was cowboying in dry-grass country. The ranchers were pretty quick to get rid of riders that smoked. Fire hazard they called it."

28

The sun was high overhead and the sky was pure pale blue without a blemish in it. Spring warmth and new life was all around them. The sap was running in the deep-booming silence. Fragrance as heavy as crushed pine needles and wild roses lay like lead in the upland air. Mark took off his black hat and let the sun dry his forehead. He watched the tracks wind ahead of them and a hard smile hovered around the corners of his mouth. Back at San Saba the sheriff would have had a ten-man posse after those outlaws like hound-dogs. Jonathon Buell was as calm and unruffled as though he wasn't on an outlaw trail at all.

"Now where; the Notch?"

"Later, maybe. Right now there's a cabin back in here I'd like to ride by."

"Squatters?" Mark looked at the broken, tortured land off on their left that the constable jutted his chin toward. There were scattered, stunted trees and gravelly soil. He reined his horse around. "Nobody but a squatter'd take up land like that."

Buell urged his horse forward with a twinkle in his eye. "A feller'd sure think so, wouldn't he."

They rode eastward until Buell cut a dim, dusty trail. Here the constable dismounted, trudged ahead leading his horse and studying the ground. Mark rode behind the constable watching the country rise up, hesitate, then fall away rearward. When he saw the log house his first thought was that it blended perfectly with its surroundings. There was a clump of scrub-oaks to one side of it that cast filigreed patterns of shade across the rotting porch. The place was picturesque, weathered, and lonely looking. The debris of such stump-ranches littered the landscape within a man's walking distance all around it. A chopping block lay amid the slash and kindling, deer and beef hides, weather-shrunk, checked, were across a broken fence.

A big, brindle hound lying full length in the luxurious warmth and dust didn't stir until one of the horses struck a rock with a steel shoe, then he sprang up in a frenzy of excitement and gave tongue.

Buell eyed the big dog askance and mounted his horse, rode into the yard with ice-chip eyes crinkled behind layers of old flesh, the pattern of hatbrim shade angling down over his lower face. Mark instinctively rode off to one side of the constable and sat perfectly motionless on his stopped horse, watching the cabin. His left hand held the reins lightly, his right hand, just as lightly, lay on his hip scant inches from the butt of his holstered hand-gun.

Buell, still watching the brindle hound, dismounted and walked up to the porch. By then a lank, slab-chested woman was standing in the doorway watching him. Without smiling but sounding like he might, Constable Buell said, "Evenin' ma'm; your husband at home?"

"He ain't." She shot it at him, looking challengingly at both of them, tilting her head a little in a sniffing way.

"Has he been here today?"

"He ain't."

Buell went a little closer to get into the shade by the porch and his expression hadn't changed. "Well," he said, "*someone* has."

"They ain't."

"Then," Buell said unperturbed, "You got a shod horse around here that sure likes to stay on the trail when he comes home. Where is he; I'd like to see a horse that smart."

"No horses caught-up but a buggy mare 'round in back in the shed."

"Is she shod?"

"No, she ain't."

Jonathon looked around calculatingly at Mark. The younger man's face was wary looking, bleak and cold. "Go take a look at the mare, will you, deputy?"

Mark went. He found an old mare greying

31

over the eyes, and doubted if she'd pulled a buggy in many a year. She was barefoot. He saw a saddle hanging from a peg by one stirrup and gazed at it fixedly. Dust was on everything in the shed but the seat of the saddle. It was clean, as slick and shiny as new money. He turned to lead his horse around front when a wisp of yellow thatch drew him back in the shadows. Ignoring the hint of movement as though he hadn't seen anything, he walked ploddingly halfway round the shed, then dropped his reins and made a lunge toward a depleted shock of hay and emerged with a fighting, biting boy no older than his own son.

He held the lad at arm's length until the fury of his attack died out and was impressed with the total silence the lad had fought in. Never once did he cry out. Not a cuss word, no sound at all. It was as though the youth fought for his life and reckoned on no outside help; feared to yell for any.

When the boy's blue eyes swung upward they had the same expression in them Mark had seen in the eyes of a spitting wildcat. Doomed perhaps but fighting and hating wholeheartedly to the very last, and beyond. Slowly he relaxed his hold on the lad's unkempt mane of yellow hair.

"You didn't have to spy on me," Mark

said. "You could have walked right out."

"Lawman!"

Mark had been called the same name with the same despising inflection many times before, but never before in quite so high-pitched a voice. He ran a slow glance over the boy and saw the bulge under his ragged shirt. With a stab, a twist and a pull he had the little under-and-over belly-gun lying flat in his palm. His dark eyes were steady, unsmiling.

"Is it loaded?"

"It's loaded."

"What's your name?"

"Carter."

"Carter what?"

"Carter Diamond."

"Where's your paw?"

"None of your business — Lawman!"

Mark broke open the little gun, used his thumbnail to eject the big .41 calibre slugs and dropped them into his shirt pocket, snapped the gun closed and held it out butt first. "Take it, Carter. Go ahead. Now — tell me something. Does your dad," he broke off, licked his lips and started again. "Tell me this: Is your paw a pretty good man?"

The blue eyes under the wild nest of hair sharpened. "Better'n you, lawman. Leastways he don't hound folks."

33

"You like him, Carter?"

The blue eyes narrowed a little. "He could eat you for breakfast."

Mark straightened up looking down at the boy. He wasn't over ten years old and he'd missed many a long overdue bath. He was wild — wilder in fact — than most Indian kids. And that gun . . .

"Come on, Carter; let's go around in front."

They went, Mark erect, burly and thick, yet with a grace to his movements, Carter just as erect in a thin-shouldered way, defiant, hating.

Buell blinked at the boy and didn't say a word until he was going up the rickety stairs to the porch, crab-like, sidling, keeping one daggerish blue eye on both lawmen, then he said, "By golly, Cart, you've grown."

The boy's mouth was pulled in thin and ugly. He said nothing. The woman glared at him. "Wh're you been, you little — "

"I watched the other one."

"And ran off at the mouth like you always do." One bony hand seemed to hang in the air a second like a hovering hawk, then it swooped down, caught the spindly youth and flung him back through the open door into the gloomy shack. Mark heard the little gun hit the puncheon floor and skitter.

Buell made a clucking sound. "No call for

34

doing that," he said. "Now — you going to tell me where Ras is or not?"

"Tell you nothing!" Her teeth clamped down hard over the last word.

Chapter Two

Mark's reaction to the woman's frank hostility was tight-mouthed dislike. He watched Jonathon Buell standing there gazing up at the cabin door she'd closed in his face and felt pity, almost disgust, for the constable.

Buell's mouth was puckered into a silent whistle when he went around his horse, swung up with a grunt and jerked his head at Carter.

They rode away from the cabin, northward, and not until they were well beyond rifle range did Buell turn his head and look at Mark.

"Tough, wasn't she?"

The mildness in the constable's voice roiled Mark all over again. "Like an old bitch-wolf," he said. "I'd have hauled her carcass in and locked her up. Waste no time on that kind."

Buell's steady eyes crinkled thoughtfully and he was silent long enough to tuck a fresh cud into his cheek, tongue it up into place and spit at a lizard on a rock as he rode by.

"That'd be one way," he agreed finally.

"Thing is, we'd have to leave off the hunt. You can't traipse all over hell's half-acre with a wildcat in tow and if we took her back to town the trail'd get sort of cold. Another thing — I sort of like the idea of her being back there."

"Why?"

Buell looked up toward Gunsight Notch when he answered. His mind wasn't occupied with the words at all. "Her old man's a penny-ante rustler. I've known that for years. Erastus Diamond. But he don't quite fit the picture I've got in my mind for either these two we're after. He just might, though, be in cahoots with them. Strangers'd have no reason for lighting out up through this country. If they weren't being chased they sure as the devil wouldn't come up here of their own free will — do you think?"

Carter studied the scaly soil, the scabrous trees, the skinny shadows and stunted grass. It was a lifeless pinch of dreariness in a land where natural beauty abounded; a man would come into it only because he had a very good reason, otherwise he'd go around it. Up through the Notch, for instance. He swung his head toward Jonathon Buell.

"You figure to swing around the shack, come in behind it and keep watch for a while?"

37

"Naw. Nothing as time-wasting as that. We'll finish tracking our boys. Maybe they'll lead us back to Diamond, maybe they won't. If they don't I can't touch him — yet. If they do — y'know — I've been waiting for Diamond to slip up for eight years."

Mark dropped down inside himself again and neither of them spoke a word. Winding their way upward into and through the trees, they eventually lost the outlaw-tracks in the pine needles and went by instinct to the breasting swale that was Gunsight Notch.

Buell reined up and got down, flexed his right leg and made a face at the stiffness, the stab of pain from its arthritic joint. He squatted down, thumbed back his hat and scanned the fall of wild country all around them.

When Mark got down he made a cigarette, lit it and inhaled deeply. His brooding glance moved a little, was snagged by crushed grass. Idly he said, "They sat here for a while." He looked out over the jagged lifts of the endless earthly turbulence frozen into rigidity, in timeless silence, and said, "Strange how men'll stop on a ridge and look all around before they go down the other side."

"Yeah," Buell said. "They saw us from up here, too." He moved his complaining right leg a little to ease it. "I figured they'd

38

do that, Mark. Figured they'd be curious about us two. That's one reason why we went in to the Diamond place. Make them think we weren't trailing them, just a couple of fellers riding. Didn't want them to think we were after them," Buell motioned toward the primitive fastnesses ahead, "or they'd have gone down into that, and if they had we'd have had a hell of a lot of riding to do and damned little chance of catching them as well." The constable stood up. "Come over here a minute."

Mark, trailing his reins, went closer, where he could see down the far side of the Notch. Buell jutted his chin. "The tracks cut eastward now. You follow them through that grass a long ways. Due east. Strange, isn't it?"

Mark squinted from behind the smoke of his cigarette, dark eyes picking out the signs of the outlaws' passing, then he hunkered down. "Why strange? Figuring they saw us turn off their trail and thought we were just travellers like you planned it — which was pretty sly at that — what's strange about them not wanting to go down into that country?" He gestured to indicate the broken up land below the Notch.

"Well — it's just as rugged the way they're doing it. Look; see the way they're paralleling this ridge we're on but staying on the north side of it? They're doing that because they want to be able to see down the Cascade Valley side all the time they're riding. Why? They saw us turn off and there's not another rider anywhere around so they don't think anyone's after them. If you and me was to rob a stage and light out with the loot we wouldn't lose time by going pretty much in a slanting direction back toward where we robbed the thing, would we?"

Mark didn't answer. His eyes followed the contours of the slag-rock and sagebrush trail over which the outlaws had ridden.

"No," Buell answered himself, "we wouldn't. Not unless we had a damned good reason."

"All right," Mark said patiently. "I'm listening."

"Unless we weren't running so much as we're trying to make a good set of tracks for a fat old constable to follow."

Mark got to his feet, stomped out his cigarette and looked up at Buell with a speculative expression. "So?" he said.

"Well, that's where relaying comes in. You take their trail from here and follow it out. Stay right out in the open where they can see you. Don't play it smart or they'll bushwhack you. Stay out in the open as much

40

as you can and dog it after them as steady as you can go. I'll go back to town."

"You'll what?" Mark said flatly.

Buell spat and tugged his hat low enough to shield his eyes. "Go back to Cascade." Seeing the coolness in Mark's face he said, "The law's like this: to make a crime you got to commit it and you've also got to *intend* to commit it. Once those two things're done, why you're naturally an outlaw. When you're an outlaw you and the lawmen sort of court one another. You, the outlaw, being stand-offish, coy-like. Me, the lawman, trying to get at you through your reserve. Well now — you're a lawman and from here on the boys we're courting get no rest and neither do you. You dog 'em and I'll go back to town and wait for them." Buell looked around at Mark again. The younger man saw the hard brightness of his glance. Buell's face was shadowed by a very faint, flinty smile.

"Why're they going back in the general direction of their holdup? Why did they come up by Diamond's place in the first place, then sashay east when any darn fool in their boots would be going north or west — and fast? Because they aren't strangers to the country like they want us to believe. They've left their sign and now they're goin' back

41

leaving us up here to get lost when their tracks peter out on a rock-ledge somewhere." Buell stretched, removed his hat, scratched his scant, greying hair and replaced the hat.

"We're going to gamble they led us up here on purpose, tried to throw us off by passing close to Diamond's place and now are riding to some spot on this ridge where they can lose their tracks in the rock. They'd only go to all that trouble because they're men who live around here, seems to me. All right. We've swallowed their bait. Now we'll do a little figuring of our own." The mild blue eyes with their extra brightness swept up. "How's that sound to you?"

Mark shot a glance at the sun, estimating the time. "I don't know," he said. "You know the country and the people, I don't. It sounds a little far-fetched but I'm willing." He hooked his thumbs into his shell-belt looking straight at the constable. "If you don't mind my saying so, Buell, you're the damndest lawman I ever ran across. The damndest."

Buell grinned. His eyes danced behind the little blobs of flesh and he laughed in a chirping, unmusical way. "A deputy from a place like San Saba, Texas, is a lot bigger man'n a constable in a place like Cascade, Arizona." Buell walked to his horse, caught up the split-reins and tugged them aimlessly through his fingers without looking around at Mark Carter.

"But a backwoods constable's got his points too. Mark — you think *you* got trouble — that woman back there, Miz' Diamond, she's never known anything *but* trouble. You'd of yanked the slack out of her you said. Well; I wouldn't have — but then I'm fifty and you're no more'n thirty. You know what makes people mean and ornery? Not having enough happiness. I figure when they've *never* had it folks shouldn't be too hard on them. Oh hell; she roiled me too, only I didn't let it show."

Mark's strong, dark face was stormy looking in a lowering, black-quiet way. In a subdued voice he said, "Why did you say 'think I've got trouble'?"

"Don't you think you have?" Buell said, gathering up the reins, tossing the right one deftly around his horse's neck.

"What do you mean, constable?"

Buell drew in a big breath and let it out. He toed into the left stirrup with his left foot. "Mark, I'm old maybe but I'm not blind. Will, for one thing. He's told me enough about you as a lawman to make you sound real great to a kid." Buell grunted, heaved, settled into the saddle and quieted

43

his horse with a big, splayed hand on his mane, reins drooping. "But to a man, Mark, it sounds — well, different. It sounds sort of ruthless." The blue eyes met the smokey dark ones. "The kid thinks you're the greatest lawman that ever lived. He should because you're his paw. But some of the manhunts he's told me about wouldn't sound too well among a group of lawmen — or any other men, I expect."

The steel-clear, brittle voice said, "Keep it up."

"Sure," Buell said, watching the still face, the perfectly motionless dark eyes. "Your wife come to Cascade alone — with just young Will. Couple weeks later you come drifting in on a spring-wind. You asked me where she lived — you didn't know."

Buell stopped talking. For a long moment they stood there just looking at one another, then Buell turned his horse and as though there wasn't anything tight and prickly between them, he said: "If I've got this figured right, Mark, you'll be back in town by midnight. I'll be waitin' for you at my office. All right?"

Mark nodded his head once, the same hushed expression on his face, in his eyes. Buell started back down the trail they'd used to reach the Notch. He didn't look back and after a time the trees with their thick shadows, their fragrant monotony, hid him, muffled the sounds of his passing.

Mark went to his horse, slipped off the bridle, tied the lariat around the animal's neck and let him graze. He loosened the cincha and made another cigarette and studied the outfall of land all around the ridge he stood upon. A big man, slouched, bleak-eyed, the sun striking the rusty flame from his hair that matched the smouldering in his spirit, in his heart.

Eileen . . . It seemed that he had never known another girl. Ever since the first dance, the first buggy ride. The blackness of her hair, the quizzical, tentative way she had of smiling. The flash of her teeth, of her wit, of her supple, strong body, the softness of her laughter. The softness . . . The softness of the thing that had grown between them. Only words now and then, not serious until he'd come back and she wasn't there. The note hadn't seemed real. Not until suppertime and the lamps weren't lit, no supper, no noise of Will, no kitchen-sounds. Then came the gnawing loneliness, the depths of despair, the shredding of his spirit. Finding her hadn't been difficult. Not for a man whose mature years had been spent in hunting down outlaws. A manhunter.

Things came back to him, up there in the cathedral silence of Gunsight Notch. Fragments he'd overlooked when he'd heard them but recalled now with no effort. Things that were like hurled stones; made him flinch now in recollection because she'd meant them . . . "Never home at all, Mark . . . Have you forgotten you have a family . . . ? I get so tied up inside sometimes, Mark, waiting for you to come back, I could scream . . ."

He crushed the cigarette, bridled his horse, tugged up the latigo, stepped aboard and reined down off the notch, skirted the worst of the shale-rock and rode eastward. Once, like a midget ant, he saw a horseman southward. Buell. He watched the creeping speck. Damndest lawman he'd ever run across. That's what he'd said and it was true. Twisted in his head some way. He talks about folks never knowing happiness, being warped by deprivation. The rest of it, too. Lawmen and outlaws courting one another. Doggondest thing he'd ever heard of.

In San Saba they'd mount a posse if they needed one and light out. They never gave an outlaw a breather and they didn't try to out-guess him. Just took up his trail and kept on it until he was run to earth. After that there was either a fight or a trial. Either way the law won. San Saba laws always won

46

— well, almost always. But this Cascade, Arizona, variety of law was different. It was funny. Its own representative would have said that. He'd have called it funny.

He lost the speck in the distance, swung back to the outlaw trail and explored the inside of his mouth and spat cotton. It was hot and he was dry. His horse had soapy-sweat mixed with dust just below the saddle-blanket; a strong horsy smell rose up.

The sky was brassy looking, more like summer than early spring. The upcountry looked to be drying out fast. When his horse plodded through tall grass, for all it was green it bent and stayed bent. It had reacted the identical way under the hooves and legs of the outlaws' horses. It was an easy trail to follow until he climbed a shallow-earthed sidehill and emerged onto a granite outcropping, like a miniature plateau where the footing was like riding over glass. There the trail died.

He made another cigarette, sitting there loose-reined, slump-shouldered, studying the brittle, windswept rock. Unconsciously he found himself adopting Buell's theory and looking ahead and south a little. If Buell was right, then the wanted men would come off the glass-rock after a while and drop south. If they did that, they'd be in grass and dust again.

Without thinking any further he skirted the granite plateau, found where a path left the rim, followed it, skirting the edge another full two hours. Then he found them again. Tracks going south through the grass.

It made him lift his head briefly, looking far ahead. Old Buell knew his country. Riding beside the tracks he wondered what else Buell had deduced from the tracks. Probably plenty. Old cuss . . . He threw up his head when the land began to dip a little, squinted out over the dazzling rangescape. It swam with sunlight and deep shadows, it was a peaceful, restful country. The kind that went into a man, stayed there. She could have picked lots worse countries.

By the time evening came Mark was still a long way from Cascade. He wasn't following tracks any more. Buell had been right. The outlaws were going back toward town. He had probably been right in guessing them to be local men, too. By the time darkness came, slowly, a solid wall of it, invisible lava smothering the land, he was riding loosely, guided by an inherent rangeman's sense of direction, toward town.

At eleven o'clock he shuffled through the dusty roadway with the sounds of Cascade around him. Splashes of yellow lantern light, dark silhouettes, smells and voices intermingled with the wonderful music of the creek that flowed just behind town. He rode erect, gaze fixed on a tarpaper shack he couldn't see at the southern end of town. All he could discern was a crooked stovepipe. A powdering of sifted dust was on his shoulders, his hat and face. He left his horse at the liverybarn and walked through the coolness, a big hulk of man light on his feet, inward, withdrawn looking. At the door he slapped dust off his pants with his hat then went inside. Buell was sitting behind his desk like a rump-sprung toad. His head bobbed up a little and the puckered blue eyes moved greasily. He made a tiny smile.

"Got her all thought out?"

Mark frowned. "Got what thought out?"

"Oh — things," Buell said vaguely. "Feller usually does a lot of thinking when he's riding alone; especially in the dark. Well — it don't matter. Their tracks come back to town?"

Mark, still looking annoyedly puzzled, dropped down on a bench. He pushed his hat back. He hadn't felt particularly tired until this moment.

"They came back to town all right. It got too dark to trail them all the way but I'll bet on it just the same."

Buell nodded with finality. His scraggly moustache glowed dark in the golden light of an overhead lamp. "Well," he said, "I expect you'll have a lot of things of your own you'll want to take care of before going back to Texas. I can't impose on you any longer but I'm sure grateful for your help, Mark, I really am."

Mark stirred on the bench. He studied the craggy old face with its ludicrous moustache and something close to indignation ran up along his nerves. "No, I don't have anything to do. Nothing I *can* do, anyway. I'll just stick around and see this one through with you."

In the same bland, unsurprised tone Buell said, "Well, now, that's mighty decent of you and I sure appreciate it." He cleared his throat. "You got a room at the hotel? If not you'd better hustle one. They're usually crowded as hell."

"All right," Mark said, pushing himself to his feet. "See you in the morning."

"Right. Oh — I almost forgot. Your kid was in this afternoon."

"Will?"

"Yeah. Wanted his old gun. Rafferty the liveryman's giving him a summer job herding horses out where the feed is." Buell's eyes twinkled. "He didn't want to take any such responsibility without his gun."

"Does he know I'm here?"

"Well — *I* didn't mention you; don't know what his mother might've told him. I expect she'd tell him though, wouldn't she?"

"No." Mark crossed to the door, lifted the bar and threw a nod back at Jonathon Buell. "See you in the morning."

He crossed to the Cascade Valley Hotel and got a room, had a bath that cost two dollars because the night-clerk himself had to haul the water upstairs, then bedded down. Evening sounds came into the room. Pale gold reflections of light danced along the walls and laughter as soft as the night itself made him acutely lonely. He lay there looking out into the frothy heavens. Now what? Stick around until old Buell had his stage robbers then drift back to Texas? Probably. He couldn't fight her; wouldn't fight her. It was wrong and he knew it, thought that she must know it too, but he still couldn't take Will away from her. Leave her to live with the deep loneliness that he carried now. He turned up on one side and closed his eyes tight. His body felt like lead — clean lead.

He didn't know when he dropped off but he knew when he awakened all right because Cascade was a change-station for north-south stages and the racket of horses, harness, hostlers hollering and wheels grinding into the roadway's dust aroused him at dawn. He thought Cascade at dawn made more noise than a town five times its size would make.

Out on the plankwalk the air was like wine, heady and clear and fragrant. The sky was pearl-grey, serene looking. The big old trees cast unkempt shadows against it in a slovenly, good-natured way. He ate breakfast and strolled over to Buell's office. Inside, Buell was nursing a cup of coffee and motioned toward the graniteware pot on the little corner wood-stove. A dolorous sound of anguish came from the cell-block beyond Buell's office. Mark raised his eyebrows. Buell made his chirping laugh.

"Him? That's Old Man Underwood. He gets drunker'n a skunk every Friday night regular as clockwork and moans like that while he's sobering up. Been doing it for years. You'll get used to it."

Mark dropped onto the bench with a wry expression. The old derelict's moanings, genuine or not, marred the morning. With a twinkle Mark said, "I suppose he's one of your folks who has never known happiness."

Buell seemed to be considering an answer, then he looked up with a light blush and combed his unruly moustache with bent fingers. When he spoke it had nothing to do with Mark's remark. "Well," he said, "we picked up their sign and tracked them back to town. Now what do we do?"

Mark's hat hid his face. He made a cigarette. "Wait until someone around here shows up flush with money."

"Is that the way you boys do it in Texas?"

Mark lit the cigarette looking across the flare and smoke at Buell, searching for sarcasm which he didn't find. "Is there a better way, constable?"

"I don't know, exactly," Buell said mildly, "but we could sort of circulate through town and see what's going on."

Mark snapped the match and exhaled. His head was back, his dark eyes intent and sly looking. He shook his head at Buell. "First off, tell me what else you figured out between the time you left me at the Notch and right now."

Buell grinned. It made his face redder. "What makes you think I figured anything out?"

"I don't know that you did," Mark said ruefully, "but you're not as simple to figure out as I thought you were. Guessing, I'd say you sashayed around and went back to Diamond's shack or something like that. You've been at this a long time and you know the people we're dealing with. I've got a hunch you've got some ideas you haven't told me about."

"As a matter of fact," Buell said, "I do have." He emptied his coffee cup and curled both hands around it leaning on his desk. "Yes, I went back around to Diamond's place. When you went around to look at that horse yesterday, was there a saddle hanging in there?"

"Yeah."

"Did it have dust on the seat?"

"No."

Buell looked into his cup for a moment. "Well — you could've saved us a lot of riding if you'd told me that." He got up and moved around from behind the desk. "Let's take a little walk."

They went down to Rafferty's liverybarn. Rafferty was short, dumpy, snub-nosed and thin-lipped. He wasn't the same man who had taken Mark's horse the day before. Rafferty had horn-rimmed glasses and a duck-legged way of walking, waddling, really. He lifted a long upperlip in a humourless smile when Buell walked in trailed by Mark, motioned toward some horseshoe kegs in the shade and dropped down on another one nearby.

"Going to be hot today, Jonathon. Hate

to see things dry out so early in the spring; going to mean a hot, turrible summer. Be cussed short feed this year. Hay'll be higher'n Tophet. I hate these early summers 'thout rain."

Buell waved a thick hand. "This is Mark Carter — Pat Rafferty."

Mark shook the damp hand and dropped it. Rafferty's shrewd grey eyes licked over Mark's heft then settled on his face.

"Say — you got a boy?"

Mark was turning away, feeling for a keg. Buell answered. "Yeah; it's his son you hired to herd horses for you."

"Oh," Rafferty said still appraising Mark's heft. "Bright kid. He can ride a horse fair too. Nice lad."

Mark remained silent. He'd known a hundred Pat Raffertys. Every town in the West had at least one. Horsetraders, sharp, calculating men who hid it all behind some kind of a mask. In Pat Rafferty it was the garrulousness he affected.

Out of a clear sky Buell said, "You still got those two horses stalled, Pat?"

"Yeah." Rafferty twisted on his keg and jerked his head down the shadowed aisle of the barn. "Last two stalls on the south side." He looked at Buell, who was standing. "You found out who stole them yet?"

Buell was unaffected. "You want miracles," he said. "Come on, Mark."

The runway was freshly raked and sprinkled. Near the rear door Buell stopped and leaned on a stall door. "Nice looking critter, isn't he?"

Mark nodded absently gazing at the big black with the tucked-up flanks. "Looks like he's had some hard use lately." He swivelled to gaze downward at Jonathon. "What did Rafferty mean about stolen horses?"

"This is one of them. The bay next-door is the other. They're the horses our outlaws rode."

Mark's gaze stayed on Jonathon's pensive profile. When the constable volunteered nothing more, appeared to be lost in a study of the black horse, he said, "Getting anything out of you is like pulling teeth."

Still motionless and gazing, Jonathon said, "When I got back last night Rafferty was spitting bullets. Someone had stolen these two horses out of his corral, rode the hell out of them and turned them loose. They come back just a little ahead of me last night."

"What makes you think our men stole them?"

Jonathon moved down farther, to the next stall where the drowsing bay, also showing evidence of recent hard usage, dozed. He

56

leaned heavily on the stall door and looked steadily at the animal. "Too bad they can't talk," he said. "I don't know for certain, but why would horse thieves steal horses, ride them for five, six hours, then turn 'em loose. Don't make sense."

Mark said, "It may not make sense to us but I'd hate to try and make a jury or a circuit-riding judge believe our stage robbers used these horses on nothing more than their appearance."

Buell turned sideways, still leaning on the door. "Would you?" he said. "I wouldn't. There were only two crimes committed in Cascade yesterday. You tracked the stage-robbers back to town. These here horses were stolen early enough to have been used in the holdup. They come in all used up just before I got back and a long time before you got back. If we figured the time out, their theft and return would mesh real nice with what we already know. I think a Cascade jury would give a conviction on that — providing we could get the men." He turned and looked at the bay horse again. "Smart, local men, Mark. Care to make a little wager with me?"

"Nope. If you're right we still don't know anything about the men." The dark eyes probed the shorter, older man's puckered

57

face. "Or do we?"

"Somewhere around Cascade," Jonathon said more to the bay horse than to Mark Carter, "there's two men who needed money pretty badly. Badly enough to figure out how to steal Rafferty's horses, rob the stage, get the bullion, leave a fake set of tracks and turn the horses loose when they didn't need them any more so's the law'd be stumped, and drop back into their old identity of local cowmen, merchants, cowboys, or what-have-you."

"Not ranchers or cowboys," Mark said. "I don't think a stockman'd risk his neck on a liveryhorse." He fished in his shirt pocket for his tobacco sack. "Where does Diamond fit in?"

Buell looked surprised, then he chirped his laugh. "Good for you, Texas. That's the key, isn't it? I wondered if you'd see it like that. The horses can't tell us a thing; the robbers wore masks — the driver and guard told me that. A perfect crime then, unless there's a weak link. Erastus Diamond might be the link. Why'd they ride past Diamond's place? Why was he gone when you and me rode out there, but his saddle, dusty everywhere but on the seat, was there?"

"Was he home when you left me and rode

back down there?"

"Nope."

Mark finished the cigarette, popped it unlighted into his mouth, slapped at a bluebottle fly and turned away, started up toward the road entrance to the barn where he could light his cigarette. Jonathon ambled along beside him.

"We could be wrong all the way around, Jonathon. Kids might've stolen those horses."

Out in the sunlighted roadway they stopped long enough for Buell to hoist a massive gold watch from his pocket and punch its stem-top. The cover sprang away from the face and Jonathon glanced at it, snapped it closed and returned it to his pocket. "He ought to be in town right now," he said.

"Who?"

"Ras Diamond."

Mark inhaled, exhaled, looked wryly at the older man's squinted eyes. "You sent for him?"

"Well — I left word with Miz' Diamond for Ras to come in this morning, I wanted to talk with him." Buell struck out, southward. "Let's got back to the rabbit-warren and wait for him. Get some coffee."

Mark walked slower. Jonathon was a few paces ahead. The taller's man gaze was over the constable's head. Fixed on the tarpaper shack that jutted forward just enough, two squares away, so he could see the front of it.

People were abroad and boys, trailed by raffish dogs, were everywhere. His eyes dropped when he heard their voices, piping-high, sometimes breathless. He noticed them all without recognising one and Jonathon Buell noticed that he noticed them, blew out his cheeks as he entered his office and expelled a rattling breath.

"Want a cup?"

"Don't believe so, thanks." He dropped onto the bench again, watched Jonathon draw off a cup, make a face because it was tepid, and crouch on the edge of his desk, more incongruous looking than ever.

"It's a long ride from that stump-ranch to Cascade just for a talk, Jonathon."

"He'll come all right."

They sat in drowsy silence for a while, then Buell put aside the coffee cup, laid his old pistol on the desk, stared at it for a moment, then began rummaging through the drawers for something to clean it with. Suddenly he said, "He'll come because I got a theory about men with consciences."

Mark's lips curled faintly. "You mean he's unhappy?"

"Nope. At least that's not why he'll come.

60

Curiosity'll fetch him. He's done a lot of unlawful things in his lifetime. He'll come to see me like a moth flies into a flame. Because he's curious as all hell. Wondering what I've stumbled onto, worrying maybe, or just plain scairt, and every bit of it adds up to curiosity. A man with a conscience has more curiosity than a cat. You watch and see."

And Erastus Diamond did come too, just after noon when the village was beginning to drowse after its bustle in the cool morning. Buell introduced the two men and Mark sat back against the wall studying Diamond. He was wispy, shrivelled, unkempt-looking with a vicious set to his bloodless mouth, a nettled sting to his glance. Mark liked nothing that he saw from the forward-tilted hat with the ferret-eyes beneath its broad brim, to the sagging old Colt's .44 that flapped carelessly at Diamond's middle as he walked and moved. The stain of a lifelong brush-popper was ingrained in Diamond. He was a weasel of a man, as treacherous as any coyote, as wily and all-knowing as a fox, deadly in a bushwhacking, sly way. He was a type and a good prototype. Mark read him right.

Buell said: "Ras — maybe you heard about the stage to Bordenton being robbed yesterday." Buell paused. Diamond remained silent. "We trailed them up by your place. To your end of the country anyway. Wondered if you'd seen anything like two strangers heading north."

"Wasn't home yestiddy, Jonathon," Diamond said nasally. "Didn't see ary a soul neither."

"Where were you, Ras?"

"Hunting caows. Stinkin' redskins been restless up there lately. Figured they might be eatin' my beef. Rode around a little just a-lookin'."

"See anything?"

"No barbecued caows, if that's what y'mean."

"No strangers? Which way'd you ride, Ras?"

"Around. North a mite, west, sashayed south a few miles too." Diamond spat the brass cupsidor, missed it shamelessly and said, "Didn't see ary a thing. Not even a redskin."

"Funny. We rode up your way yesterday and saw a big village on the move."

"Which-a-way was they goin'?"

"East."

"I didn't ride over that-a-way, Jonathon. Figgered there wasn't n'need after I seen most o' my caows was safe 'nough."

"Maybe your missus saw the outlaws go by."

62

Diamond's eyes crinkled. A chiding slyness came into his voice. "Y'asked her, she told me. She gets a mite short when she's snuck up on. I reckon you found that out."

Buell smiled a little. Seeing the constable's smile, Diamond made one of his own. It showed badly discoloured teeth. Buell said, "Yes, we found out she don't hanker to have folks surprise her all right. By the way, Ras, you want to sell that saddle hanging in the lean-to out back?"

Mark, watching Diamond's face, thought a brief shadow crossed it. Diamond shook his head. "Dassn't, Jonathon, 'tain't mine."

"Wilson saddle, isn't it? Whose is it?"

"Yeah, it's a Wilson. Belongs to a feller hunts wild horses in the plum thickets along the upland creeks. 'Breed feller."

"What's his name?"

"Mac. His name's MacCargadel or some such a damned thing. I never could hardly say it, let alone remember it. I just call him Mac."

"Is he mustanging now?"

"Yep; been out about a month. Since the weather let up a little. I expect he'll be coming in pretty quick now." Diamond cocked his head to one side and said, "Y'don't suspicion him of robbin' your stage do you, Jonathon, because I can tell you he didn't do it."

"That's so, how?"

"How," Diamond said, "for one thing he don't never come to Cascade nor the valley parts. He's a 'breed and stays back in the hills. You know them kind, Jonathon."

"Yes, but that doesn't mean anything either, Ras. Lots of folks don't like towns — in a pinch any of them might rob a stage."

Diamond said, "He just wouldn't have, that's all. You're wasting your time."

"I might be but whoever did rob it rode past your place and out over Gunsight Notch. Why would they do that, Ras? If they were strangers they'd stick to the good travelling country. If they were looking for a place to cache their loot and knew the land why I reckon they'd pick the end of the country up around your place — don't you?"

Diamond mumbled a short answer and stood up. He watched the constable. Buell just leaned back in his chair and thanked him for coming in. Ras Diamond left and Buell turned to Mark.

"What do you make of him?"

"For one thing he's a liar."

Buell's eyes crinkled. "That so? How's he a liar?"

"He didn't see any Indians. If he'd been hunting his 'caows' to the west he'd of run

64

smack into that village we saw. If he rode north he'd of been in the hills and would have at least seen their dust and if he rode south he'd of cut their sign if he rode by after they'd passed."

"Yep," Buell said, "I figured that too."

Mark wasn't finished. "If he was looking for his cows so hard why did he keep away from the open country below the Notch?"

"You tell me."

"I'd guess it this way: He either knew enough to stay clean away from there or else he rode over there and met the outlaws. In either case he naturally wouldn't want to say he'd been there. If he didn't know about them and was looking for cows why'd he avoid the grass country up there? That'd be the first place any cowman'd look for his cows — where there's grass, not trees."

Buell arose, wiped the oil off his cleaned gun with a rag and dropped the old weapon into its holster. He puckered up his eyes at Mark in a disarming smile. "You know, I expect even Texas deputies can see the light now and then." His teeth shone startlingly white in their bushy setting. "You think we got a link?"

Mark shrugged as he stood up. "There's one around here someplace, maybe it's Diamond. But I'd of kept him here — gotten it all out of him."

"Naw you wouldn't have," Buell said. "Because we knows there's more'n one and if we scairt one the other'd take off like a bird."

Mark snorted. "You don't think Diamond'll run and tell his friends — maybe this 'breed — you had him in here for a talk?"

"Sure he will. Why'd you think I kept saying they might be strangers and that we tracked them as far as Gunsight Notch? So he'll tell them we took their bait. That we're barking up the wrong tree."

"You made it strong enough about his 'breed."

"Not that strong, Mark. I dropped it when I could but I didn't dare act so uninterested."

Mark was frowning a little. "And Diamond'll ride 'way back up there in the breaks again and when we want him we'll have a hell of a time getting him out of those hills without a posse."

"Hope not," Buell said mildly. "Besides, I don't have funds for posses. Maybe we can work on his curiosity and get him to come to us if we want him again." Buell regarded Mark thoughtfully for a moment then said, "Let's take a walk down to the stage company. They'll want to know what we're doing."

Mark reached up and pulled his hat low as they left the office, and around his upraised arm he said, "If this works out like I've a notion it's going to I won't be around long enough to get to know these people here."

Buell belched *sotto voce*, cleared his throat and said, "You never can tell about things like that, Mark. You never can tell."

Chapter Three

The elder partner in the stage company was a brusque, impatient-eyed man of sixty or so. In short sentences he snapped out answers to Jonathon and Mark. It was obvious he was as much irritated by Buell's calmness in the face of his company's loss as he was at the loss itself. When Mark asked about the bullion he got back a whip-like answer.

"Of course we take every precaution, Mister Carter, you understand, but there's no way to make a stage foolproof. We do all that we can. From there on it's in the lap of the law. We pay enough municipal taxes, Lord knows."

Irritated a little Mark said, "The law's limitations are the same as yours."

"How's that?"

"The law does everything it can too, but it isn't altogether foolproof either. The law has to depend on what people tell it *after* a crime's committed. Sometimes folks have private reasons for not telling what they know. Other times they just plain don't see things at all."

"Humph! Seems to me," the stage company owner said with a bleak look, "you two'd be better off out looking for the robbers than standing around in here asking questions."

Jonathon spoke soothingly. "We've looked, Charley. Looked to hell and back but we can't manufacture outlaws for ourselves."

The stage owner bit off the end of a cigar and spat with more vehemence than was necessary. "There're enough of them running loose nowadays, Jonathon. I think what Cascade needs is younger lawmen."

With a level, dark gaze Mark said, "I can see where you'd have enemies. Can you tell us who you suspect of robbing you?"

The cigar smoke lent a strong, pleasant odour to the warm office. The eyes above it fixed themselves on Mark in a steady, disliking way. "If I have personal enemies, Mister Carter, that would be my business, not yours. As for the robbers, I imagine they aren't local people. I've met stage robbers in my time. Men who travel over the country robbing, very seldom striking the same place twice."

"Have you been held up before?"

"Of course. I've been in this business thirty years."

69

"When was the last time, and where?"

"Last time was just below Bordenton at the northern end of our local short-line. Five months ago. They got three thousand dollars in vouchers and four head of good team-horses."

Mark let Buell carry the balance of the conversation. It dwindled and they left the office. On the plankwalk Mark twisted up a cigarette, lit it and smoked in silence. Buell gazed southward over the town.

"Well, Texas, what do you think of him?"

"Him?" Mark said. "I don't think much of him but that wasn't what I was thinking about. Tell me something, Jonathon. When his line was held up before — those four horses came back home, didn't they?"

Jonathon's eyes twinkled in appreciation. "Right as rain," he said. "You're coming right along."

A sharp look from the dark eyes and Mark said, "What do you mean by that?"

"Nothing. Listen, I've got to go fetch the mail and run an errand or two. Come on back to the office after dinner and we'll hack this thing out. All right?"

Mark watched Buell walk in his heavy, rolling way straight down the plankwalk until he was four doors south of the office. There he turned into the Cascade Valley Mercantile

70

Company and Mark's gaze drifted farther down the roadway, stopped at a scraggly geranium bed beside a tarpaper shack, and his feet began to move.

The sound of his own footsteps was loud in his ears, matched the quickened beating of his heart until he raised a fist to knock on the door.

Eileen Carter opened it and looked startled. "I thought you'd gone."

"No." He took off his hat and entered the room, looked hopefully around, but they were alone. "Where's Will?"

She seemed to draw herself more erect, search his face without answering.

"I just wanted to see him, is all."

"To take him, Mark?"

He shook his head, holding her eyes with his own. "No — just see him."

"He's out playing. He's made friends fast, here."

"Sure. He's a likeable kid, Eileen. Always was."

"I thought you were going back, Mark."

"No, I didn't say that. Eileen — "

Her eyes were troubled, liquid looking. "Don't say it, Mark. It's all over."

"I don't believe that," he said slowly. "I just plain don't believe that. Listen, you tell me what you want and I'll — "

"You can't change, Mark. If you could you'd *know* what you've got to do, you wouldn't have to ask me."

"That's not right," he said doggedly. "Eileen — I'll mail my badge back to Jim. Send along a resignation with it."

Her eyes grew darker. "Didn't you resign before you came here?"

"No. Took a leave of absence that's all."

"Do you see, Mark? You *can't* stop it — that manhunting."

"Wait a minute. I didn't know I'd have to quit."

"That's what I meant a moment ago. You'd know what it would take for us, Mark, if you could change, but you can't. Manhunting is like — like whiskey is for some men to you. I've heard that said before but I didn't believe it. Oh, but now I do, Mark."

"That's silly," he said, with the first showing of irritation. "I'll send back my badge and resignation today. I can get a job driving stage, I expect. Maybe shoeing. I used to be pretty good at that. Hell, Eileen, I'll quit sheriffing right now — today."

Her shoulders lost some of their erectness. "Mark, you ought to know all I ever wanted was a normal married life and healthy home environment for Will. Not guns and manhunts and posses all the time." She turned

72

abruptly away from him, stood looking down at a small crate-table and spoke standing like that, back to him. "Have you eaten, Mark? I know you haven't; you never do unless someone makes you. Sit down."

He sat. She fed him and after a while she sat down across from him and drank one cup of coffee. It was the least desired, most uncomfortable meal he'd ever eaten in his life and he was conscious of the silence between them while he forced the food down. When he was finished he made a cigarette and lit it.

"All right. I'll quit. I'll — better yet, you can write out my resignation now. You can mail it back with my badge in it."

She was watching him, seeing the way his thick mat of hair curled up over his ears from the pressure of his hat. The way lines were chiselled into his cheeks and down both sides of his mouth. It wasn't a face that smiled often. The crow's-tracks up around his dark eyes from squinting down long trails.

"You waited so long to do this . . ."

He studied the tip of the cigarette. "I didn't think those little arguments we had went that deep, Eileen. I missed out there, didn't I? I always figured someday you'd see there's got to be law and lawmen. I just thought you hadn't grown up enough to understand."

"I grew up, Mark. I grew up just enough not to want to be a widow or to have a son, an orphan, grow up to be a lawman and do the same thing to some other woman."

He looked at the cigarette. The old thought came back but he didn't say it. "Lawmen? There are worse things."

He got up heavily with a sombre lightness in his heart. He went around the table thinking her defences had given away so easily, really, when he'd have sworn upon entering the shack she was just as adamant as ever. It was strange; funny, as Jonathon Buell would have said.

She arose to meet him. He kissed her. The pressure of his mouth was soft, her lips were cool, like velvet, full and ripe. She pushed back against him and stepped back, looked into his face.

"Mark — I'm sorry. I'm sorry, dear. I know you like the work, how you feel about outlaws and the laws, all the rest of it, but we come first. You and me and Will. Our family, our love. See it from my side, Mark. All I want is you and happiness."

He took the little nickel badge from a pocket and tossed it on the table between them, stood gazing at it. There was a bitterness in him he couldn't — wouldn't — hide. Then he raised his shoulders, dropped them and looked at her.

"You'll write the resignation? I'm not very good at letters. And send back the badge."

The little house was stifling. He went over to the door where he'd dropped his hat and retrieved it. Eileen hadn't moved. "I'll do it, Mark. I'll do whatever you want me to do."

"Well," he said, looking at his hat. "We can't go back to Texas, to San Saba. An ex-lawman is a pretty unpopular critter."

"We can stay here. It's beautiful country. I loved it the minute we got off the stage. And Will has a job at the liverybarn herding the loose-stock. You can get a job, too. We can stay here and do right well, Mark."

"Yeah," he said absently. "Well — I'm going for a walk, Eileen."

"But you'll be back for supper. Will doesn't know you're here. I didn't tell him. I thought it wouldn't be fair; tell him you'd been here and gone away."

"Yeah," he said again, then he slapped his hat on and squeezed the door latch. "I love you, Eileen."

"Mark . . ."

Outside, the sun, miraculously, was gone, and in its place were high thin clouds scudding fast southeastward. There was a hurrying little breeze that rode a foot off the ground and cooled Cascade without stirring the dust. He noticed it, felt it against his face and heard it lisp under his hatbrim. A spring rain coming, he thought, as he walked northward automatically.

A man finds his niche, and that in itself was no small thing, then he has to relinquish it. Not that he wouldn't make as much money as a stage driver, he would; might even make more, but that wasn't the issue.

He sighed, trudging stolidly through the worried coolness with it breaking out around him with whispering sounds. Well; it was done. Maybe you didn't ever get much happiness without paying for it. He turned in at the constable's office with a crooked smile. Happiness. That was Jonathon Buell's word, not Mark Carter's. Buell wasn't far off though; a man would fight hard for happiness.

"You look like you swallowed a bittersweet."

Mark sat on the bench and shoved his big legs out in front of him and gazed at his boot-toes. "I did. A bitter-sweet."

"We all do now and then."

Buell was going to say something else but the door flung inward and Pat Rafferty was there. A gust of cool, damp-smelling air came in with him. Mark and Jonathon both looked up. Rafferty's eyes were bulged. At sight of Mark a stricken look crossed his face. Buell's surprised glance was bright.

"Spit it out, Pat. You look like you seen a ghost."

"I —," Rafferty's eyes flashed to Mark again, then jumped back appealingly to Jonathon again. "I — been robbed again. Two more horses stoled, Jonathon — but that ain't what counts . . ."

The wind came into the silence, brushed over the building leaving a blind heaviness in the office's atmosphere.

"The kid . . ."

Mark's body was motionless. Buell leaned forward, staring at Rafferty. "Go on," he said softly. "The kid . . ."

Mark put both hands on his knees and pushed. Stood up watching Rafferty's white lips with a drowning sensation inside him.

"They killed the kid."

Buell came up slowly. Of the three he made the only sound. A broken, irregular expulsion of breath. A dozen or so big, fat raindrops fell on the roof.

"Some of the horses come into town. I and a hostler saddled up and rode out where Will said he'd be takin' the animals. There he was . . . The horses were scattered. We — brought 'em back and corralled them. There were two missing again. The kid was — "

"Where is he?"

"Due west about six miles. Him and the horse he was ridin', both."

Mark was out the door first. He trotted to the liverybarn and got his horse. When he jogged out into the roadway Jonathon was waiting there. They rode into the lowering gloom. Buell looked up once, squinted and sniffed. Mark didn't raise nor lower his glance but held it steadily westward. His face was grey.

With the miles ticked off rearward Buell was swinging his head constantly, reading the horse-sign when Mark veered off and lifted his horse into a fresh gallop. The shadows were low, the sky leaden, the little breeze gone. A hush lay deep over everything.

Buell dismounted when he came up, stood in deep silence. They were down together. One of Will's boyish legs was pinned under the horse. There was more than enough to see. Buell studied it all before the dark shadows thickened and the rain came — if it cam — to wash it all away forever. There was the terrible sight of a kneeling father in the greyness, beside his dead son.

Mark only spoke once, that was softly, when he touched his son's face and called his name. Buell, hearing, twisted, straightened up and held his eyes on the dead horse. That was when he saw the bullethole and the powderburn around it. He went back over to his horse and waited with both arms thrown across the seating-leather, chin low, eyes looking steadily, unseeingly, back toward town, away from Mark.

"I'm ready, Jonathon."

He was on his horse with his son in his arms. Buell took the lead so Mark's horse would follow. They went all the way back to town like that and when they pulled in at the liverybarn there was a mute, still crowd waiting. Jonathon waved them off and Rafferty made a mistake. He stepped up beside Mark and said:

"Here; let me give you a hand."

"Get away."

He dismounted and walked through the crowd like it didn't exist. Walked to the doctor-undertaker's, shouldered through the door and stepped into a gloomy-cool environment that was like the old man who owned it. The doctor looked into Mark's face and away.

"On the little table over there. Fine. What's his name?"

"William Benton Carter, age ten years."

"How did it happen?"

Mark's big hand was on the boy's shoulder, his eyes looking down. "Gunshot," he said. "Murder."

The doctor licked his lips. "You're Mister Carter?" He got a nod. "Where can I get in touch with you?"

"Through Jonathon Buell. I want him put down well. Not fancy — nice. Comfortable."

"Yes. I understand. I'll send you word."

Mark went back outside. Up the road someone was beating a dirge on a piano and lanterns were coming on here and there. It wasn't evening but the black clouds cut off daylight. The hush persisted, uneasy, as though the earth and everything in it was waiting. It would storm. A shadow pushed off the front of the doctor's house and said:

"She knows, Mark."

He turned. Jonathon's outline was there, the moustache hanging low in the dismal light. "How do you know she does?"

"She was at the office a minute ago. I came here to catch you before you went to see her."

"Why? What business is it of yours?"

"Mark — she's broke up; bad off. I sent word for my missus to go set with her. Leave her alone for a day or two."

He thought: *She blames me.* Aloud he said, "It wasn't my fault, was it?"

"No, of course not. Give her time, son. A couple of . . ."

He plunged off the boardwalk and crossed through the gritty dust to the far side, stepped up and turned south. At the little shack he raised his fist, held it aloft and saw that the door was ajar, lowered it and pushed. The door swung inward. The room was empty. There was a feeling of loneliness, of grief, in the air. She wasn't there. He stood irresolute a long time then the drops began to fall, their coldness streaked across his face. He turned away leaving the door open and went back northward again. Past Jonathon's office and didn't see that Buell's door, also, was open, and that Jonathon was staring out of it, watching him. Past the mercantile, the blacksmith shop and into the liverybarn. Rafferty wasn't there. A hostler came up dryeyed, silent.

"Saddle my horse." The sound of rain, the smell of it, prompted him to look down at the man. "You got a slicker here?"

"Sure. I'll fetch it."

Mark's hands hung like dying birds at his sides. He moved them, made a cigarette and hung it in his face, lit it and took the reins of his horse when the hostler came back.

"Here's the slicker."

He took it, shrugged into it, found it three sizes too tight and ignored that, lay one big hand on the upthrust butt of his forward-slanting carbine and looked at the hostler. The man's mouth was partly open, his eyes were dry, unblinkingly steady on Mark.

He rode out without speaking. The hostler followed him to the doorway where a slanting drizzle was turning the dust to mud and there he saw the big man on his big horse turn shiny under the rain-lash, riding northward. Heading up the Bordenton trace the same way he'd originally come riding into Cascade.

The uplands shed water well and the rain hadn't been coming down long enough to make a mire out of the road. Mark left it when he was in sight of Gunsight Notch, felt the soil turn stony, gritty, underfoot, and let his horse follow the twisting, ragged little trail toward Ras Diamond's place.

Through the shaggy trees his figure loomed large and rain-ship with big sloping shoulders under the too-tight slicker. His hatbrim cascaded water down its open front, past the up-curling edges and its blackness was made darker by water. His face was grey-impassive, only the dark eyes showed a flickering vestige of life, and little things were bubbling through the shocked state of his mind. Little things from ten years back; little pictures and little sounds, but there were no feelings evoked by the memories, just the shock that blocked off everything but the smell of the rain-enrichened earth. The sound of wind-song in the overhead, through the gaunt, struggling trees. The remembered sounds of an unseen boy's laugh, his voice . . .

A hound howled in the stygian blackness ahead. His mind reached for that sound, closed down around it. Diamond's brindle dog. He reined up and listened, gauging distance and direction, the things that came naturally to him to do; came instinctively to him out of the developed senses of a long-time manhunter. He dismounted heavily and tied his horse back off the slatternly trail in the trees, clumped through the mud with the hound's baying in his ears and enough of the shock gone for him to orient himself in the darkness. He made a slow swing to use the roundabout shadows then he saw the bulking shape of the cabin and a pale swath of lamp-light glowed weakly but steadily from one window.

The hound was beside himself. The scent was strong and knife-sharp. It was also disturbing. The animal loomed, stiff legged, hackles up, head held low, baleful yellow eyes fierce and glassy, fangs drooling, slobbers mixing with the rainwater against the mottled earth. Mark only glanced at the hound once; he waited.

"You there, Gen'l — shut up yore damned tonguin' or go chase 'em — one or t'other."

The thin silhouette was off to one side of the thin ribboned light behind Diamond where the door was partially closed. Mark took four more steps. Grey, murky paleness limned him.

"Diamond! Come down here!"

He couldn't hear the gasp but he saw the thin chest buckle, raise quickly and fall.

"Who's out there? Come up closer."

Four more steps and he was within ten feet of the rotting stairs to the porch. Diamond's head went lower, his neck stretched, little mean eyes stabbed futilely against the rain darkened gloom.

"Who is that? Consarn it, man, come closer."

Mark didn't move, just his right arm. It crooked, a hand snaked in under the slicker, came out with a black gun that burned glossy-blue in the tortured night.

"Come down here, Diamond. Come down here or I'll kill you right there on the porch!"

Diamond's silhouette hung forward in awkward stiffness. He could make out the cocked gun but the man behind it was just a hulking, shiny outline with water running off him.

"Now!"

"What the hell . . ." But Diamond came, thin shoulders hunching up when he left the porch's protection and the stinging rain pummelled him. He cursed when he slipped in the mud. Closer, close enough for Mark to see his face, Diamond stopped, peering intently up into the stranger's face. Recognition came swiftly. The vicious mouth drew flat.

"What you doin' — drawin' a gun on me?"

Mark pushed back the slicker, dropped the gun into its holster and moved still closer to Diamond, hooked the thin man's arm with his left hand and propelled him farther away from the house, into the dripping shadows by the trees where his horse stood on three legs, watching.

Diamond twisted in the grip, crooked his head and looked up. Faint light shone off his face. His mouth was open, no sound came. Still holding the wiry arm Mark swung him facing.

"You lied to the constable, didn't you?"

"No. Who the — "

Mark's wet palm made a cracking sound against Diamond's face.

85

"Why did you lie about not seeing any Indians yesterday?" His voice was steady, unhurried, like the slamming palm he struck Diamond with a second time. "Why?"

Diamond cursed. The hand came up again. Diamond's head snapped under the impact, rolled and wobbled, his pale eyes in the damp sheen, in the fear and fury, were unblinking, wide.

"I'll kill you, Diamond. I'll strangle you right here, right now. Why did you lie?"

"You got no right to do this . . ." It trailed off, the big hand struck again, harder. Diamond sagged, fell sideways, held up by the big fist closed around his arm. Dazedly he groped for his gun. Mark struck it from his numb fingers. It fell in a pool of water.

"Why did you lie?"

"You can't do this."

"I *am* doing it. I'll kill you, Diamond. I'll kill you like I'd kill a scorpion and think no more of it. Why did you lie?"

"I had to. I — met two fellers — "

"Who were they?"

"I never seen 'em before. One was ridin' a black horse, t'other a rawboned, big bay horse. They — "

"You'd recognise them if you saw them again?"

"No, I wouldn't. They was in the forest

up towards the Notch. It was shadowy and they caught me off-guard. Was in the brush with guns when I rode up."

"You're lying again, damn you. You'd have to see their faces."

"No — not through the brush. Gun barrels was about all I seen. That's gospel truth."

"What did they say?"

"For me to go back to my place, leave my horse and walk out in the woods behind the house. They'd trail me back. If I tried anything they'd shoot me."

Mark looked down into the bruised face, let his hand drop away from Diamond's arm.

"Did you do it."

"Yeh. I turned my horse loose, hung up m'saddle and went out back. The old woman didn't even know I was back. Nor my kid. I went back into the trees. They was waiting."

"Go on; quit stopping."

"One of them give me this —," Diamond rummaged through his sodden clothes and came up with a gold watch on a chain. "He said it was mine if I'd set up on a hill and watch for the law, and when it come ridin', if I'd draw it off."

"You didn't do that, Diamond."

"No," Diamond said protestingly, "you're damned right I didn't. I told them I would

87

then I just hid out in the woods until dark and went back home."

Mark shifted his weight, heard the squish as mud oozed out around his soggy boots. "What did you see about them, Diamond? You don't talk to them, stand with them in broad daylight and not see something."

"They kept back in the brush that first time, north of my claim. Second time they was in amongst the trees; shadowy back in there."

Mark's hand came up, his thumb hooked in his shell-belt. "You saw something. What colour shirts were they wearing? What kind of guns did they have? How'd they wear their hats?"

"The guns — they was Winchester .30.30s — carbines. Everybody's got — "

"What kind of clothes?"

"I couldn't see much. They was careful. The big one never even — "

"One was taller than the other?"

"Yeah. One was about my size, the other one was over six feet. Big, skinny feller. Wore a seal-brown hat. The little one did all the talkin'."

"What kind of a hat did he wear?"

"Black. Big one, like yours. Black Stetson, I'd say. He had corduroy pants, sort of brown looking, with buck-skin sewed on the inside of the legs and around the seat. Saddle breeches."

"Was he masked?"

"They both was. Black masks all over their damned faces."

"What colour shirts?"

"Regular old blue work-shirts as near as I could tell."

"What kind of a voice did the shorter one have? Deep? High? Young or old?"

"Young voice. I'd say they was both young fellers. Shorter feller's voice sounded pretty common."

"Would you know it if you heard it again?"

"Well; I don't know. Nothin' unusual about it."

Mark heard a noise and raised his head. Diamond's lank wife was silhouetted against the doorway light peering out; she held the latch in one hand behind her.

"Give me that watch."

Ras Diamond handed it over. He seemed relieved to be rid of it.

"Diamond — if they ever come back and you tell them I was asking about them — I'll come back to see you again."

"Won't say a thing. Nary a word." Diamond's courage was returning. There was a fight going on inside him, it showed in his eyes, in the jutting thrust of his mouth. "You got no right to touch a man to get information. That's the law, mister."

Mark pocketed the watch and brought his head a little lower, a little closer to Diamond's face. "I'm not the law, Diamond. I'm not even a deputy, you understand? I just want to meet those two outlaws. They're loose somewhere right now. They may have robbed another stage and they may come riding up here again. If they do and you don't tell Buell about it — and I ever find out you've protected them — I'll kill you. Don't forget it; I'll kill you."

He reached up and spun Diamond by one bony shoulder and gave him a hard shove. The rain was drumming with increasing intensity. The wind soughed in the treetops. Diamond stumbled, slid and skittered to his porch, turned part way, head twisted, saw that Mark hadn't moved, and plunged on up the stairs to the porch. When he turned a last time, shivering, soaking wet, in the warmth of the shack's doorway, the shiny-slickered hulk of Mark Carter was gone.

He rode parallel to the sluice-running roadway into Diamond's place, going back toward town. The ground was slippery now, like obsidian. His horse walked head-down, eyes puckered against the gusts of wind that carried rain like tiny fists against him.

The town lay huddled under a lashing wind when he rode through its splashed roadway, the old trees bending, posturing, making dismal sounds, but the rain had been momentarily blown away. He and his horse were alternately sharply revealed and plunged into blackness as he rode through the lantern beams from the houses and saloons.

Inside the liverybarn's draughty runway the horse gathered himself up stiffly and shook so hard the stirrups flapped grotesquely. The hostler was watching Mark when he reached for the reins, received them and was left standing alone.

Jonathon was in the office. He looked up, expressionless, his eyes alive but his features tired and sagging. Mark didn't sit down, he towered over the constable and the desk, water ran off him in steady rivulets.

"Whose watch is this?"

Buell took it, smoothed the water off its face and studied it. "I don't know," he said. "Where'd you get it?"

"From Diamond. Find out if it's the driver's or the guard's. Who got robbed this time?"

Buell's head rocked back slowly. He put the watch down, leaning back in his chair. "Same line. Twenty-seven hundred dollars in government payroll money. Horses came back again."

"Where did it happen?"

"About three miles north of the last one. It's too — "

"Do you know two men around Cascade who pardner together, one as tall as I am, maybe a couple inches taller, and one short, about Diamond's size?"

Jonathon's face grew thoughtful. He was silent a long time. "Well — it isn't a matter of pairin' up two like that, Mark. It's a matter of pairin' up two who *might* be the right men." He looked up. "I'd rather not guess at all than have two innocent men shot, boy."

Mark's unwavering stare hung a moment, then he turned without another word and walked out of the office, closed the door and stood in the gusty night. There was something in its wildness that found response in himself. Something dark and deep and turbulent. He saw a tall man come out of the saloon across the road, teeter on the plankwalk, undecided. Not wanting to see people right then Mark nevertheless stepped down off the walk and slogged through the mud. The man across from him watched as he approached, kicked the mud off his boots on the edge of the walk, and stepped up.

The saloon's light cut down across the tall man's face diagonally. He said, "Hell of a night," and Mark looked up sharply, saw the green glint in the stranger's eyes and shouldered past him without speaking.

The saloon was full of people, mostly men. Cigar smoke hung thick except when draughts caught it, twisted and wrenched it cruelly. Noise, like the rain, beat against him and fell away. He went far down the bar, around the bend where it joined the wall, hooked an elbow, just stood there, watching people drift past, losing himself as hard as he could in the bedlam.

Chapter Four

When he couldn't hold his eyes open any longer he went upstairs to his room, shucked the slicker and threw himself upon the bed, muddy boots and all, and fell asleep. When he awakened the sun was high, torpidly hot, and steam arose from the earth without a breath of air to disturb it. The last rain until Fall. Spring, gusty, unpredictable, was over. Summer would work its golden embroidery and bleaching heat from now on.

He shaved and washed and went downstairs, past the cafe and across to Buell's office. A wispy man with a kind face and perpetually narrowed eyes was smoking, sitting on the bench holding in his hand the watch Mark had taken from Ras Diamond. He nodded when Mark entered. Mark nodded back.

Buell said, "Good morning. This is Jock Andrews. It was his watch you got. Jock — Mark Carter."

"Howdy."

They shook.

"Howdy." Andrew pocketed the watch and remained standing. "Well," he said to Jonathon, "like we said, that makes around seven thousand they got, if it's the same two."

Mark was watching Andrews. "One of them was about six feet tall and the other one was about your size — five eight or nine."

The driver's quiet glance moved back to Mark's face. "When they nailed me they was hidin' in the rocks." He seemed to turn something over in his mind. "It ain't much to go on is it?" he said. "The world's full of men who're either six feet tall or shorter." He nodded to them both and left. Buell got up, went to the stove and poured two cups of coffee. Over his shoulder he said: " 'Bout gave you up. Been saving this coffee for our breakfast."

Mark accepted the cup, held it watching the steam arise. "Did you go see the other stage?"

"Yeah, before dawn. The same — same — system, was used."

"Modus operandi."

"Yeah. Where'd you learn that, in Texas?"

"No, I heard a Pinkerton say it once. Not much doubt but that it was the same fellers again."

95

Buell sat down and shook his head. "Nope I don't think there's any doubt about that. What crossed them up was your boy. They didn't expect to run into a herder with Rafferty's horses, I guess."

Mark drank the coffee and said nothing. He hung the cup on a nail over by the stove and went back to stand above Jonathon's desk. "Tell me something; do you think they're men from the range or men from town?"

"Why," Jonathon said, "you answered that yourself. Stockmen wouldn't run a risk like that on livery animals. They'd be townsmen then, wouldn't they?"

Mark watched the older man's face. "What did you figure from going out there this morning?"

"Not a hell of a lot, Mark. Just that I'm surer than ever we figured it out about right the first time, up there on the Notch." Jonathon's eyes dropped, contemplated the coffee cup in his hand. "Andrews, that stage driver you just met, told me something. A Cascade rowdy named Darrel Timmons got jugged over in Bordenton last night. Andrews heard it from one of the deputies who rode out after the stage was robbed."

"So? Who's Timmons?"

"A sort of local no-good." The blue eyes

96

came up. "Big, skinny feller. Used to be a swamper around town for local freighters. Andrews said he got drunk and troublesome over there; they tossed him in to sleep it off."

Mark kept his eyes on Jonathon's face for a long time. The warm smell of the drying outdoors was in the room with them. The summer smell. Somewhere close by a boy was laborously whistling to a dog. The sound was high, unmusical, and reminiscent. It wavered, lifted, broke and began all over again. Mark's eyes were still, with a moving shadow in the depths. He reached for his tobacco sack, dropped his head low and worked over a cigarette. Buell watched him. When the thing was going, smoke drifting up, he said: "On a bender, eh?"

"Yeah. Darrel's a shiftless sort, always has been. I knew his folks years back. They moved on. Darrel came back to Cascade about three years ago."

"Big, skinny feller on a bender. Pockets full of money."

"I don't know about the last."

Mark watched Jonathon. "You suspect him, don't you?"

Jonathon squirmed in his chair. "Mark; it isn't suspecting him that's worrying me. It's you. Have you been to see your wife yet?"

OUTREACH SERVICES
Waterford Public Library
5168 Civic Center Drive
Waterford, MI 48329

"She blames me — you know that."

"No, I don't know any such a thing. You're the one that said that, not me."

"I don't want to see her right now."

"Man," Jonathon said a trifle exasperatedly "now's the time when you *should* see her. Woman-grief is a lot different than man-grief." He put his empty cup on the old desk, pushed it back. "We're getting away from what I started out to say. Suppose Timmons isn't one of them. The way you're thinking right now nobody could convince you of it. If the Bordenton law turns him loose and you find him — I know Darrel pretty well. I'm getting to know you, Mark. There's going to be a killing. That's bad enough if he's guilty. It's a darned sight worse if he isn't. See what I'm thinking?"

Mark turned and walked out of the office, went down to Rafferty's and sat on a horseshoe-keg, spoke to the day-hostler without looking around at him.

"Fetch my horse, will you."

People passed him by on the plankwalk, looked and quickly looked away. The horse came, he ran a finger under the cincha, found it snug, turned the horse, toed in and sprang up, rode out into the drying mud of the roadway with the sun dazzling-bright, took the stage road north and held a steady pace over it. Several times he met travellers, nod-ded when they nodded. Once a stage lurched by. The drying ground was spongy, the heat humid-hot.

Bordenton was at the end of the road, down a last, long-rolling swale where the road flung itself exhaustedly out of the hills onto the grassy floor of another, wider, valley. It was a newer town than Cascade. There were no trees except in the middle-distance where hills rose like stairsteps, reddish-purple. The sun shimmered over the place, struck the erectness of the buildings, oozing sap, and fell back eye-stingingly so that Mark pulled his hat lower to shield his eyes as he rode into the southern end of the wide road-way, wove through a curling serpentine of mid-day traffic, horses, buggies, wagons, and sought the liverybarn. He left his horse there to be grained, washed-down and hayed, and went heavily back as far as the local con-stable's office.

The room had three men in it. The air smelt of green-pine, of newness. It was a raw little building set slightly apart. The constable acknowledged Mark's self-introduction and introduced him to his two deputy consta-bles, both young, hard-looking men who nod-ded, gripped his fist briefly, then dropped back into watchful waiting, studying the big stranger, feeling the aura of violence that hugged him, permeated the office emanating outward from him.

"You have a man locked up here named Darrel Timmons. I'd like to talk to him."

The constable looked more relieved than disappointed when he answered. "You made a long ride for nothing, mister. We turned him loose about an hour ago. He was only in until he sobered up, y'see."

Mark blinked solemnly, shuffled his feet a little. "Where did he go. You know?"

"Well, I'd guess he struck out for Cascade. That's where he's from, the boys tell me. Uh — did you come all the way on the stage road?"

"Yes."

"Did you meet a tall, thin feller on a leggy sorrel horse?"

"No," Mark said, recalling each traveller he'd passed.

"Hummm. Well; maybe he didn't head back then." The constable looked at his deputies. "You boys got any ideas?" They didn't have. The constable shrugged resignedly. "Golly; I don't know how I can help you, mister. Y'see, Timmons don't come around here very often."

"How much money did he have on him when you took him in?"

100

The constable's eyes stayed a moment on Mark's face before he answered. His shoulders hunched forward a little as though he was about to get out of his chair. "He was pretty damned well fixed for money, I can tell you. It's a wonder he didn't get knocked over the head flashing it like he was doing."

"A lot, eh?"

The constable spread his hands. "Did you take a look at that stage held up late yesterday afternoon south of Bordenton?"

The constable's shoulders hunched still farther. He stood up, his eyes shiny. "Yes. All three of us rode out there. The cussed rain drowned out anything like tracks we might've found. It was a real shame. Are you hinting Timmons got his money off that stage?"

"I wish I knew," Mark said. "I'd give a thousand dollars myself, just to know." Three sets of eyes were fixed on him. No one spoke. He went to the door, hesitated, nodded at the lawmen and went outside.

Walking toward the liverybarn he considered the question of the stolen horses. When he went into the manure-tainted atmosphere and found the day-man, he began questioning before he even said his own name.

"Do you know a rider named Darrel Timmons?"

The hostler pinched down his forehead in

concentration, then gave it up. "I might, mister, if I seen him, but so damned many fellers come in and go I never bother with half their names."

"Well; he was jugged last night for being drunk and disorderly. Tall, skinny feller, not too old. Had a wad of money on him."

"Oh — hell yes. Timmons, eh, I didn't know his name but I recollect the man now. He got out in the middle of the road in the rain last night, singin' fit to bust. Night-constable told him to pipe down and he got troublesome. Night-constable rapped him alongside the head and took him in. Sure, I remember him. I helped drag him into the lock-up. What about him?"

"What kind of a horse was he riding?"

"Sorrel with a flaxen mane and tail. Flashy critter; pretty sound, too, what I recollect of him."

"Any brands?"

The forehead pinched down again, then the hostler wagged his head regretfully. "By golly, I didn't look. If he had any I don't remember seein' 'em. I'm sorry, too. I usually make it a point to look at brands. Was he a horse-thief?"

"No. At least not as far as I know. I'm just trying to find him."

"Oh," the hostler said, not at all convinced

Timmons wasn't a horse-thief. "Well; when he got out this morning he got his sorrel and rode off."

"Which way?"

"South."

"On the Cascade road?"

"Yeah."

Mark nodded. "Thanks. Now, is my horse cleaned up and fed?"

"He's cleaned up and grained, but he's still eatin' hay."

"All right. I'll let him finish it. Where's a good place to eat?"

The hostler threw up an arm. "Over there. Rose's place."

"Thanks again."

He crossed through the curling heat of early afternoon indifferent to the wondering stare behind him, entered Rose's Cafe, crossed the small room in two strides and dropped down on the bench in front of the smooth, slab counter.

The woman who came through the curtain separating the kitchen from the dining-room was of mixed blood. She had liquid dark eyes, large and soft and warm looking. They went to Mark's face and stayed there, neither friendly nor unfriendly, just looking, appraising.

"Fried potatoes," he said, "and fried meat and coffee."

She nodded and disappeared through the curtain. The place was empty except for him. He gazed out the window, saw the flow of leisurely traffic under the heat-scorch, heard town-sounds, clangour of anvil, rattle of chain-harness, men's voices, dogs, and while he looked and unconsciously heard, he thought about Timmons. If the man had ridden south like the liveryman had said, then he left the Cascade road somewhere en route south. Where? Why? Not knowing Timmons made it hard to guess.

"There you are. Two bits."

He turned back toward the counter, dug out a quarter and handed it to her without looking up, without seeing the kindled interest in her warm gaze at him. And he ate.

Where? Why?

At Diamond's cut-off. It came to him so easily, so naturally, he stopped chewing, sat perfectly still considering it. Diamond had talked to the men. One was tall, over six feet, the other was about — about Diamond's size. He laid down the fork. Timmons went south and turned off the stage road somewhere before he got to Cascade. Plausibly, he'd cut off at Diamond's roadway. Why? Why, because he knew Diamond; had something to see him about. Why would that be? Because he and Diamond were the outlaws?

"It's too rare?"

He looked at her blankly, then looked down. "No, it's fine." He picked up his fork and ate some more, then he laid it aside for the second time and picked up the coffee cup, tilted it, drained it and saw her over the upraised rim leaning back, hands behind her on the pie table, smiling at him, her body arched. It was like a pail of ice water being dumped over him, what he saw, sensed. He arose hastily, stepped over the plank seat and left. Crossed to the barn and got his horse, saddled, bridled, mounted and rode out, going south.

It looked better to him as he rode through the afternoon with the sun on his right side. Even if Timmons and Diamond hadn't done the robberies together, at least Timmons, a suspect, was going to see Diamond. Diamond would talk to him. Mark would find out what they talked about.

He shook his head to still the tumbling thoughts. Maybe Timmons hadn't turned off at Diamond's road, too. Perhaps they didn't know one another at all. It might all be wrong. Not all. Not the part about Diamond because he kept cropping up one way or another. He knew something, he had to. Jonathon had said Diamond was a small-time rustler, a no-good. He'd also said the same thing about Darrel Timmons, the tall, skinny man. There was something there; something . . .

The shadows lengthened and the earth seemed to sigh as the heat lessened. Once, a big, bulky cloud, all fluffy-white and dirty grey at the edges, rolled in front of the sun and coolness came briefly, then it was gone, sailing serenely across the flawless blue. It wasn't ever quite as warm again that day.

Where the Diamond cut-off was, Mark stopped for a moment looking at the ground. There were three sets of horse tracks, all shod. One went in and out and one just went in. He thought about it. Someone had ridden into Diamond's place and out again. Timmons? Probably. Someone else had ridden out by the same road and apparently hadn't returned, at least they hadn't returned by the same route. He rode across the road, out a ways, found no other tracks and rode northward several hundred yards and swung west paralleling the road in among the scraggly old trees toward Diamond's cabin.

And there he was discovered.

"Lawman!"

Mark started, hauled back and sat motionless.

"Sneakin' around in the trees. Thought you'd slip up on us, didn't you?"

106

He looked into the wildcat eyes with their spitting expression, their abiding hatred raw and as clear as ice, as sparkling. He ignored everything but the sixty pounds standing straight-legged in the gathering shadows. Everything but the boyhood.

"Howdy, Carter."

"Don't 'howdy' me — riding in here so's the trees'd be between you and the house."

The dark-still eyes hardly moved but they saw the battered rifle, the bulge under the filthy shirt where the belly-gun snuggled. "Out hunting?"

"F'rats — yeah. Sneaks that come slipping through the shadows."

Mark sucked in a big lungful of air and let it out slowly, eased forward, kicked his right foot free and stepped down. Standing beside his horse, right hand hooked by the thumb in his shell-belt, left hand trailing the reins, he was a mountain next to the tousled-headed mole-hill.

"Hunting deer?"

"I told you what I was hunting."

Mark wagged his head slowly. "Yeah," he said. "You told me. But that's like the wind in the treetops. That's just air." The dark eyes were pensive, quiet looking. "Deer're hard to hunt afoot. I hunt a-horseback, myself. Saves your legs and if you get one you've got something besides your back to fetch him back on. Ever snare a deer?"

No answer. The sullen-spitting look stayed up, stubbornly. The boy hadn't moved. He was half-poised to fight, half-poised for flight.

"Someday, maybe, I could show you how to do it. Once I caught a cinnamon bear in a buck trap. That sure was a mess. Another time I was out with — a boy — about your size and age — and we snared two wild turkeys. Texas wild turkeys. There's nothing better, roasted. Any wild turkeys in these parts."

"No."

"Should be," Mark said, looking at the trees and back to Carter Diamond's face. "This ought to be good wild turkey country. I'll bet there're some back in those hills. Up by the Notch."

"Indians're up there — well — somewhere back in that country. It's not a good place to go."

"Yeah," Mark said softly. "You know, when I wasn't much bigger than you are I lived with some Indians."

"What kind?"

"Comanches, Texas Indians." He could see the boy's adams-apple bob up and down.

"Comanches?"

"Yes," a thin smile hovered up around

the dark eyes. "You look like Comanches are something you wouldn't like to meet."

"I wouldn't," Carter Diamond said swiftly, the last vestiges of wildness leaving his eyes, wide open now, looking wonderingly at the big man. "Not Comanches — golly, no."

The smile hovered, gathered strength. "Aw," Mark said, "you've been listening to old women talk."

"No I haven't," the boy said emphatically. "I've heard *men* talk. They said there's nothing worse than a Comanch' Indian. Nothing — not even a grizzly."

Mark moved his feet, stood hip-shot. "One time," he said, "I took a Comanche's spear away from him and beat him over the head with it. I've still got that spear — back in Texas. If you want it I'll send for it and you can have it."

The boy was at a loss. His mouth hung open a little but no words came for a long time, then he said, "Honest?" Almost whispered it.

"Honest."

"Golly."

Mark squatted in the little clutch of trees, his spurs making a soft, tinkling sound, and draped the reins over one big leg. The boy's sharp, smudged face was mellowed by the dying daylight, the descending shadows.

"Wish you and me could be friends, Cart," he said.

That brought back something. He saw it pass over the lad's face, settle in his clear, bright eyes. Not like before but it was there all the same.

"Seems like every time we meet you're itching to pull a gun on me. Why's that — no foolin'?"

"Well — you're a lawman."

Mark sat stonily for a moment before he replied. "No I'm not. I used to be, sure, but I'm not now, and even if I was, Cart, did you ever stop to think what the world'd be like if there wasn't law in it? It'd be a poor place to live; every man's hand against other men. Why, you wouldn't dast be out here hunting right now; the woods'd be full of other hunters — manhunters, plunder-hunters, women-hunters, raiders — be like it was when the Indians ran the show. You'd never know when someone was going to shoot you off a horse from behind a tree. See?"

"I reckon," the boy said, leaning, relaxed and fascinated, on his old carbine. "Only — you dog my dad, too, and that's hunting, isn't it? You and Old Man Buell — old Goat Whiskers."

Mark's eyes twinkled softly, richly. "Whoa," he said. "That's no way to talk. Mister Buell's a fine man, Cart."

"No, he ain't."

"Do you know him?"

"Well — "

"Ever go ridin' with him or huntin' with him — anything like that?"

" 'Course not," Carter said stiffly.

"Then you don't know him. You've got to be with a man a while to know him. Go hunting with him, if you really want to know what kind of a man he is. No — you've got Constable Buell all wrong."

"Why's he hound our place? Why'd you fellers slip up on my maw and me the other day? That wasn't friendly, was it?"

"To tell you the truth," Mark said, "maybe it seemed like we slipped up but didn't either of us have that in mind when we rode in. Honest." The blue eyes were doubting. "Cart; if we'd meant to slip up, we wouldn't have come on the road, would we? We'd have come through the trees."

"Like you're doing now?"

Mark was stopped. To cover up he fished out his tobacco sack and began to make a cigarette. He'd had a rule for ten years. You never lied to a child. It had led him into some near-disasters but he'd stuck to it.

He lit the cigarette and broke the match. "Yeah, Cart. Like I was doing just now."

"Are you after my dad?"

A tough one to answer. A near-lie was the same as whole-lie. "I was looking for a tall, skinny feller on a flashy sorrel horse with a flaxen mane and tail."

"Oh, him. You mean Darrel Timmons?"

"That's right."

"He was here. Long time ago. Before I even went out hunting. He ate dinner with us."

"Where was he going when he left you?"

"Down to Cascade."

"Did your paw go with him?"

"Naw. Paw went out looking for cattle. This time of the year they drift a lot. Paw says it's because of new feed. He saws cows're all right. They'll come home in the Fall when the feed's gone, but you got to keep watching steers. They got no homing instinct; keep on going."

"I know," Mark said, standing up. Timmons *had* turned off at the Diamond cut-off. He *had* talked to Erastus Diamond. Good; so far so good, but there was still that one single track. "Cart; anyone else stop by your place today? A neighbour maybe, or a traveller who's still at the house?"

"No. There's been no one around. Why?"

"Well; I saw the track of one horse on the trace."

Carter's straw-coloured hair caught the last droplets of daylight and held them imprisoned in its tumbled thickness. "That must've been my paw. He was out all night. Does that now and then when he's looking for our critters. If he's too far off come evening he beds down in the back country and comes in the next day."

"Oh — sure," Mark said, studying the thin face, the high, bony shoulders. "That'd account for the tracks all right. Does that every now and then, huh?"

"Yeah. You know how cattle wander."

"Sure," Mark said again, snapped his reins and pulled his horse in closer. "Well, I reckon I'd better get down to town, Cart." He mounted and sat up there, thick, massive-looking, looking down into the pale upturned face. "Sure glad we're friends, Cart," he said softly.

The boy was abashed and showed it for the first time. His lips moved. "Me too. You — won't forget that spear, will you, mister?"

Mark moved his head back and forth. "You've got my word on that, Cart, and say — my name's Mark. My last name's the same as your first name. That's strange, isn't it?"

The boy nodded, his eyes shining in the

dullness. "You going to the house?"

Mark ran a big hand along the jut of his jaw. "I don't think so. I'll head back to town. S'long, Cart."

"S'long, Mark."

He rode with the pleasant night beside him and the memory of a dirty face whose mouth had made an unconscious Oh! and the distant memory of a Comanche lance standing in the dark corner of a Texas Ranger outpost. Other memories came crowding. Things that could winnow the numbness out of a spirit darkened. Times of soft summer evenings in another place, all softened with a shade of pathos. The faces of two boys much alike. The grave but wavering sound of a lad's earnest efforts at whistling. All boys whistling at all the raffish, grinning mongrels in the world, and somewhere a man who would shoot a boy whose belt held a hammerless old pistol with the big walnut butt showing. And somewhere else a woman's face . . . It always came back to that. *Man, now's the time when you should see her!*

He made another cigarette and exhaled from down deep with his head thrown back and the last glory of a bloody sun reflecting off the planes of his face. An azure streamer was high overhead, tinged turquoise, soft and cornflower-blue. The blue of a girl's eyes in Texas years ago. A hundred, a thousand long years ago, each year a lost yesterday. In the distance an anvil clanged mutedly and two dogs barking rapturously came into the solitudes to join him as he sloped downward, breasted the last lip of land and cut cross-country into the north-south stage road.

Cascade lay soft and drowsy with just its upper ramparts touched by the last ruddy light. Lower down shadows hung like grey lace, in careless folds, around the buildings, the people. Somewhere, down there, was a tall thin man and a flashy sorrel horse.

The liveryman was poking gummed mud out of the spokes of a yellow-wheeled rig when Mark rode into the gloomy runway and dismounted. He straightened up, cautious little eyes going, first, over the horse, then over the man. A tentative smile lifted his lips. Rafferty laid the stick carefully on the buggy's step and rubbed his dirty hands along his trouser-legs and came forward through the dimness. Without speaking Mark handed him the reins. Rafferty caught a short glance at the big man's face, noted there was something there beside the harshness, the congealed coldness of yesterday.

Mark went through the coolness to Jonathon's office. The constable wasn't there but the door was unlocked. He went in and sat on the hard old bench, leaned his shoulders against the wall and let the shadows gather, thick and pleasant, around him. He was still sitting there, hidden in the dinginess when Jonathon came back after supper, lit the lamp, strained to hang it on the overhead hook, saw Mark's eyes on him, unmoving, and gave a startled grunt.

"You — gave me a start." The blue eyes probed. "Had anything to eat lately?"

"I ate over at Bordenton. They turned him loose this morning. He came back over this way. Stopped up at Diamond's for a spell. Have you seen him around Cascade, Jonathon?"

"I haven't looked for him," Jonathon said slowly, turning his back on Mark with a guilty feeling inside him. "You don't often see a man like him unless you *do* look for him." Buell perched on edge of his desk, swung one leg idly regarding the whisker-stubble, the red glow of wind and sunburn on Mark's face, and said, "Was Ras Diamond the other one — do you know?"

"I think he was but I can't prove anything at all."

"Did you go by his place?"

"Well — yes. I didn't hunt him up though."

Jonathon looked puzzled. He kept swinging

his leg. "If you was up there . . . ?"

"I met his boy."

"Oh."

Silence closed down between them. After a while Jonathon got off the desk, went around it and sat down. "Doc's holding the services Monday morning at eight. Your wife — you see, you weren't around — your wife said it'd be best about that time of the day."

"Where?"

"Cemetery," Jonathon said. "It's south of the house she lived in, about a square."

Mark got up. "I went by her house. She wasn't there."

"Well, no," Jonathon said, looking down at the desktop. "She's over at our place."

Mark studied his face. "What does she say?"

Jonathon spread his hands. "Not much, I reckon."

Still watching Jonathon's face Mark said, "No place for me, is it?"

"I wouldn't say that, Mark. It's been your place — at her side I mean — since it happened."

"You know better'n that."

"No, I don't."

Anger, as clear and sharp as a bell rang in Mark's next words. "Then why don't you look me in the face when you talk?"

Jonathon's head came up, his eyes were sombre, steady. "Listen, Mark. I told you couple days ago your place was at her side. If you think differently I got no business telling you different. You're hard to figure at best. I'll be blunt with you, boy. The lad's gone. Chasing someone you think killed him isn't going to fetch him back. A woman — a mother — is broke up but, instead of you going to her like most folks would do, you leave her to strangers in a strange town. I can't figure that out, personally."

Mark got up, crossed the room and went out into the lazy smelling twilight. He hesitated, teetering on the edge of the walk, then crossed the road and entered the saloon he'd been in before. It was supper-time, not many men were abroad. The barkeeper nodded amiably at him, knowing who he was like all Cascade knew, made his mental wager too, like all Cascade was doing, and said nothing; showed nothing on his face.

"Beer."

It came, cool and tangy. Mark drank it, ran the back of his hand over his mouth, dropped a coin on the counter, turned and walked back outside again.

Night air with a stain of chill in it washed the heat out of his face, encircled him, held him with a loose enfoldment. The beer worked its subtle tranquillity too. He made a cigarette, smoked it leaning against the post he'd seen the green-eyed man by the night before and let the loneliness, the emptiness engulf him. When the cigarette was low he turned, re-entered the saloon and when he leaned on the bar the keeper smiled a little and set another beer in front of him.

"Where does Jonathon Buell live?"

"Live? Well, he lives around the square, south. The second house. There's a picketfence around it and an old dog in the yard, usually. But he — "

"Thanks."

He walked south and turned left at the narrow opening where houses stood in drab, sentinel rows on both sides of a drying roadway. The dog was there, but if he wasn't blind he almost was, for when Mark went through the gate and it squeaked, the old beast hobbled over and snarled at it ferociously.

He went to the door, removed his hat and rapped softly. The answer was slow coming. A short, almost square woman opened it finally with a tired, drawn expression. At sight of Mark her eyes widened uncertainly, something like hopefulness in their depths.

"I'm Mark Carter; can I see my wife?"

The woman stepped aside and pointed across the living room. "Out there, Mister Carter — on the sun-porch."

He crossed the room with unreasonable urgency, as though he wished to make up for a wasted day. The sun-porch was balmy and dark. Standing in the doorway, filling it, his hatbrim crumpled under one big fist, he probed the shadows until he saw her, far down at one end in an old rocker.

"Eileen?"

There was no answer. The dim figure didn't move.

He went toward her, tossed his hat on a willow sofa back against the wall.

"It's Mark, Eileen."

The rocking-chair made a slight sound as though its occupant had turned, was looking up the darkness.

He went up beside it and down on one knee, feeling for her hands. "Eileen. I — don't know what to say."

"There isn't anything to say, Mark," she said so quietly he hardly heard. The tone, the words, were hushed, low. He tried to catch an inflection, any kind, and there was none.

Her face was a pale outline only. There was no way to tell what it held. She was erect in the chair yet relaxed. What disturbed

120

him the worst was that she didn't move, scarcely breathed. Diffidently he sought her hands, like stones in her lap, cold, unresponsive.

A murmur of voices came from within the living room. A lamp flickered to life, some of its pale light tumbled through the window onto the sun-porch and Mark saw how white her lips were, how dark-rimmed her eyes. His heart faltered. In the softness she was the girl of sixteen he had once known in Texas. Inside him, it hurt. Abruptly she spoke.

"I'm glad you're back, Mark."

For a moment he was puzzled. Back, yes; had she doubted he'd come back? Something like a rare illumination, something almost like intuition said *No, she means she was afraid for you.* He tightened his grip on her hands but one worked loose, lifted and felt for his face. It was cold, the touch seemingly impersonal in its chilliness.

"Mark?" There was a leaden softness to her voice. "Did you have to go? That's it, isn't it; you had to."

He didn't know what to say, what to do, exactly. There was a barrier between them, something he couldn't tear down with his arms. He wanted to reach for her, draw her close, but the invisible obstacle was there.

"You know what happened, Eileen."

"So — you got on your horse and went after them. Did you find them, Mark?"

"No. I will though."

Her head nodded forward just the smallest bit. "Yes, you'll find them. You've never failed, have you?"

He tried to see her eyes but she was profiled to him. Baffled, totally adrift in this environment, he said nothing, just knelt there in the weak light with a hollowness, an ache of spirit he'd never felt before.

"We're a long way from home, Mark, aren't we?"

"We'll go back, Eileen. If you want to go back we'll go back."

The chair squeaked again. She dropped her hand from his face and looked around at him, downward. "I didn't mean Texas, Mark, I meant home. Home is where the heart is. We're so far from that."

He closed his throat against the thickness that was suddenly there, big and solid.

In a voice that sounded like a small wind rustling ashes, he said, "Eileen — we were happy. You and Will and me, we were happy."

"Will was always happy, Mark. He missed you very much, too. I — shouldn't have . . ."

"Don't talk about it. Don't blame yourself."

"But I'm to blame, I think. It was self-ishness, wasn't it, that made me run away from you. Made me want to bring him up in a gunless world. I wasn't facing reality, was I?"

"Someday there won't be guns, Eileen."

In his own head the echo was strange. He believed in guns, had always believed in them. There *had* to be guns, he'd said it a hundred times. There had to be guns to enforce laws, to make people realise that the law's retribution was too high a price to pay for doing unlawful things. Now he didn't talk that way. He looked at the floor, wondering; thinking *I'm not being honest am I?*

"Mark — did you . . . will he have a nice — box?"

"Nice," Mark said emptily.

"He was your son, wasn't he? Did you know he had a gun, Mark?"

He looked up at her. "Yes, I knew. I didn't think you knew."

She began to rock a little, very slowly, very gently. "I've been smelling gun-oil since I was a little girl. It was on his clothes. Did you see it, Mark? I wish I could have shared that with him. His secret."

"The constable gave it to him. Mister Buell. It was an old gun with no firing pin."

"You'll keep that, won't you?"

Perspiration came to his upper lip. Something a little like panic seized him. What had become of it? An old gun . . . She wanted to keep it. "I'll keep it," he said almost in a whisper.

She was silent a long time. The chair rocked, making a soft, abrasive sound, then she spoke again.

"Mark — we're so far, far apart. Will gave us what little we had, you know."

Something stirred in him. The opening of doors leading into infinite darkness. He was falling — losing something. With an effort that choked him he flung out his arms. The chair stopped moving.

"We've always been close, Eileen," he said. "Now we're closer."

"No, I don't think so."

"Yes — "

In the same quiet-emotionless way, as though she had been wrung dry of grief, she said, "Don't you see Mark; it's finally happened. Manhunting drove us apart. Now it's between us and I know you can't help it any more than I can help how I've always felt about it."

"No. Eileen; you have my badge. You were to send back my resignation."

"We were too late, I think." She bent a little to see his face. Her full mouth was

124

loosely held, it was shaped to no expression at all; a sort of numbness lay across it. "Coming here was our crisis, I think. Now it's over."

"It's not over," he said, fighting back the riot of words, of feeling that rose up to pierce her strangeness.

"It's all over but your part of it."

"My part?"

"Yes. You'll hunt them down. You'll kill them, won't you?"

"Eileen." The name sounded strained even to him. "Will was our boy."

"Of course he was," she said in that same dead-sounding way. "Of course. It's only right that his father go after his killers, isn't it?"

"Eileen!"

She turned away from him, looked back into the night again. The rapport between them was broken; a great-surging silence built up in the shadows. He got slowly, heavily to his feet and his spurs rang.

"Eileen. If they went unpunished — don't you see?"

She started to rock again, very silently. She was deaf to him and he knew it, felt it, but the suffocating helplessness hadn't gagged him like it would, yet.

"It isn't just for Will, Eileen, it's for every

boy who's herding horses somewhere." He stopped with his mouth still open and the hopelessness came, closed her off from him. He stood like that for a minute longer.

As though from a long distance, she spoke. "Will killing them make it all right?"

It was the old, old difference again and he was powerless to fight against it now as he'd often been in the past. He stood there dumbly knowing he shouldn't have allowed things to progress as they had. He'd come to her to offer his heart, his solace. Now . . .

He went back into the living room and Jonathon Buell was standing by a window looking out into the front yard. He turned when Mark's spurs rang behind him. A tight look up around his eyes made him look even older than he was. A dead cigarette hung from one hand. Softly he said, "Supper's about ready, Mark."

Mark shook his head, ran one hand over the other hand, doubled up. The skin was rough, the hand unsteady. In a strained tone he said, "I'm doing this wrong, Jonathon. I — can't — just can't get the feel of it. She's out there — my wife. I — I — don't know."

He left the house, went through the gate and closed it, turned right and walked without being aware of doing it, to the corner of the square, turned right again and stepped up onto the plankwalk that existed on either side of the main roadway only. A sighing little wind broke around him, going south. He sensed other walkers without seeing them. After the little zephyr was gone a stillness settled. He crossed the road toward the liverybarn, anglingly. Plodded through the night to its lantern-lit maw, and there he told the night-hawk to fetch him a livery horse. Let his own horse rest.

Chapter Five

The horse was an ugly seal-belly brown with a hammer-head, a mean little eye and toughness built into him to match his looks. Mark noticed it and understood the thought behind it. The hostler knew he wouldn't spare a horse, had given him one that couldn't be killed. He took the reins and started to turn, to toe into the stirrup. Another horse, in a tie-stall across the way, caught his eye. It was gloomy-dark, what lantern light there was, fell weakly, but the stalled horse's mane and tail showed pale.

He stood like a crane, one leg on the ground, staring, then he withdrew his leg from the stirrup, put the foot down solidly. The hostler was watching him, puzzled. He held out the reins, the hostler took them. He went around the brown horse and into the stall adjoining the tied animal, leaned over the partition and looked long and hard at the beast. When he walked back where the hostler was, his eyes were as hard as glass.

"Whose horse is that sorrel with the white mane and tail?"

"Uh — belongs to a feller named Timmons."

"How long's it been here?"

"Timmons rode it in this afternoon. I'd say around four o'clock."

"Where is Timmons now?"

"I don't rightly know, Mister Carter. He just sort of comes and goes." The wary face turned, craning upwards. "He don't seem to have no steady habits like most of us."

"What saloon does he hang out in? Where does he live?"

"I don't know where he lives. Used to have a shack south of town but last I heard he was workin' for some cow outfit back in the hills. He hangs out in the saloon across from Jonathon's office, mostly, I reckon. I've seen him in there, anyway."

Mark was moving toward the door when he spoke. "Tie that horse up. Leave him saddled and bridled. I may not want him."

He went through the darkness swiftly, crossed the roadway and entered the saloon. Men's voices, like the droning of a saw through water-logged wood, hummed in his ears. The tobacco-smoke broke around his face and the barman, swabbing the counter, lost a stroke at sight of his face looming up close. Their eyes met and held.

"Which one of these fellers is Darrel Timmons?"

The barman leaned on the counter, puckered up his face and made a slow circuit of the room with his eyes, then shook his head. "I don't see him in here right now."

"Was he in here?"

"Yes. Couple hours or more ago. He had a couple of drinks. I don't believe he come back though."

Mark's disappointment was acute. He saw no evasion in the barman's eyes but he turned his back, leaned on the bar and studied the customers. Some might have fit the description he had, but he felt the barman had told the truth. He wasn't conscious of the accruing silence in the place until he pushed off the bar turned back and caught the barman's eyes riveted on him. He beckoned him closer.

"Who're Timmons' friends; you see any men in here he pardners with?"

Another firm headshake. "Timmons don't pardner much, Mister. He drifts in and has a few drinks, sometimes sets 'em up for the house and that's about it. Oh, a lot of these fellers in here now know him all right, but I wouldn't say any was friendly with him."

"Lone wolf?"

"Not exactly," the barman said, making mechanical motions with his bar-rag. "He just ain't a feller folks seem to cotton to very much." The man's eyes came up. "Kind of cocky feller."

"Where does he live?"

"That I don't know." He looked past Mark's shoulder and jerked his head. "I'll find out for you."

A grizzled man with a fierce walrus moustache, curled up Texas-style, to resemble the wicked horns of a Long-horn, came up beside Mark and leaned forward, eyes fixed steadily on the barman. "Yeah," he said in a guarded way.

"Where's Darrel Timmons live, Tex."

The weathered, ageing face turned slowly to regard Mark. The blue eyes were smokey looking. "South of town. Shack with a horse-rack in front of it five doors down from where your missus lived, Mister."

Mark studied the face, it was hard and sharp, watchful more than unfriendly. The man knew who he was; probably the whole damned town did by now. Word like that travels fast. "Thanks," he said, and walked away from the bar. Then, the silence struck him and he recognised it. Cascade knew. Knew who he was, what had happened, and was betting on what the outcome would be.

He walked south through town, found Timmons' shack, forced the door and left a trail of burnt matches behind him. There was nothing there. Timmons hadn't been back to the shack in a long time, maybe weeks. Mould on uncovered food, the smell of the place, told him that. He began at the southernmost store that was still open and made a very systematic search for Darrel Timmons and never found him. It was late when he gave it up. Wherever Timmons was, he must have gotten word, for there was no trace of him anywhere. He went back to the liverybarn heavy-footed, saw that the hostler had been watching his progress and stopped squarely before the man.

"Timmons come for his horse yet?"

"No. It's strange he ain't, too — by now."

"Why's it strange?"

The man made a weak gesture with one arm toward the buildings across the road. "He must know you're looking for him by now, Mister. The news would get around."

"Yeah," Mark said. He went over where the brown horse was, untied it and led it near the road-entrance of the barn, brows knit. There, he stood looking out at the town, at its darkness, its liquid gutters of damp light, the men who were standing in little groups here and there, smoking and talking.

He could go back and ask Jonathon to lock Timmons up on suspicion. He could wait by the horse, or he could do what he'd originally intended to do; go up to Diamond's and try to catch Diamond out a ways — do what he'd planned to do earlier, before Carter Diamond had made it seem bad to do it — tear the truth out of Erastus Diamond. Kill him.

If Timmons knew, he wouldn't come back for his horse more than likely. The dark eyes flickered. And if Mark was right, Timmons wouldn't even try to get his own animal; he'd steal one, because Mark knew, now, that he'd been wrong about the stage robbers. They hadn't been townsmen, exactly. They'd been men who knew Rafferty's horses well enough to know which ones to steal, to risk their necks by using in their robberies, and that fitted a man like Timmons to a T. He'd know every good horse out of Rafferty's herd. Without more thought he swung up and nudged the ugly horse out into the night. Timmons was probably hiding or riding hard by now; he'd have to let him make tracks and go after Diamond — unless Timmons was heading for Diamond's place right now — in which case . . .

He lifted the brown horse into its slamming lope as soon as he'd climbed past the sloping land beyond town. Held him to that punishing gait until the beast's breathing was a cross between a gasp and a whistle, then he allowed him to settle into a loose-jointed Spanish running-walk. He alternated speed and recovery like that until the pine fringe at Diamond's turn-off loomed up, then he walked the beast three quarters of a mile west and left him tied in the trees, went back afoot and studied the turn-off. There were no new tracks. If Timmons was coming, he'd either come a different way or Mark had beaten him. Good.

He had to get down on his hands and knees to see the tracks and there was none, other than those he'd seen earlier. Brushing the crumbling, flinty soil off his hands he went back through the trees until he could see the lighter blackness of the cabin's outline against the moonless blackness of the night. There was a lamp-glow spilling out across the rickety porch. Remembering the brindle hound he made an extra wide circuit and came upon the rear shed from the west. Inside, the mound of loose hay reflected a moist kind of light all its own. He used this to examine Diamond's saddle and saddle-blanket. The blanket was clammy but it was dry. The saddle had a fine, almost invisible coating of dust on its seat. It looked as though Diamond hadn't ridden out after he'd come back that morning.

A more thorough investigation disclosed a leggy, spooky-acting bay horse in a pole corral off the shed's south side. The animal had rolled in the mud. Gobs of it hung, dry and tan looking, to his belly-hair.

One horse, a dry saddle-blanket, dust on the seating leather; Diamond was around. Good. He stood in the deep shadows behind the house knowing that he'd never get Diamond out again like he had the night before. Not now, not again. His head moved a trifle, the dog might be around in front. If he was he probably wouldn't scent Mark. He hunkered, skimming his gaze along the ground, trying to skyline the house area because this time he didn't want the dog to give him away. There was no sign of the animal so he stood up and moved silently closer, went all the way up to the cabin's thin, splintery wall and flattened there. Abruptly he heard the sharp cursing of a man. The words singed the air, exploded in harrowing gasps of profanity being used with great feeling. A woman's tones came next, reprovingly, waspishly. Her words held Mark motionless.

"Well — y'asked fer it, y'fool."

"If I was able I'd fetch him back and hang his gawd-damned hide on the corral. I'd skin the dirty little whelp alive."

"What'd y'have to take on so, for? Now I got it *all* t'do around here." There was resignation and whining complaint both, in her voice.

"I don't care — it's the horse, y'old scut."

"Y'can track him come daylight, now hold still."

Diamond let out a thin peal of anguish and settled down to sizzling cursing again. Mark hung there listening, his own breath and heartbeat loud in his ears. The conversation assumed a closeness, as though whatever they were doing absorbed their attention entirely. No further reference was made to their son. Mark waited, willing them to come back to the topic, or just any topic, but they never did.

He slipped back to the shadows by the barn-of-sorts and pieced sense into what he'd heard. Carter had taken one of Diamond's horses and left; had run away. Well, that wasn't surprising. Mark, staring through the night at the back of the house remembered Diamond's words and a new trouble came into him. Diamond would trail the boy come sunup. The ground was just right for taking horse tracks now. Dry enough and not too dry. Diamond, undoubtedly an old hand, wouldn't have much trouble; he'd catch Carter all right.

Mark retreated into the trees farther, squatted down and made a cigarette but didn't light up, just sucked on it. Sat on a boulder and kept his vigil. But Timmons never came. No one came and the hours went by unseen, unfelt, until just before dawn when the cold, sharp fingers crept along the earth, then Mark knew Timmons, if he'd run, had fled without warning Diamond. He stood up stiffly, flexed his stiff muscles and started in an even large circuit around where the ugly brown horse was. He wanted Diamond; he'd get Diamond. But Diamond would trail young Carter therefore Mark must find the boy first. After that all he'd have to do would be to wait with the boy for the man to show up. It would work out fine. Especially since he wanted Diamond alone, off-guard, and a long way from his ranch. Wanted to kill him.

The brown horse wasn't even stiff, which further attested his toughness. By the time Mark had ridden back and forth, quartering, for over an hour and had found the tracks of a ridden horse going due west, the dawn was breaking.

He struck the trail and held to it until he

broke out of the stony, juniper-studded flat land and saw an eminence, wind-swept and barren, ahead. He rode part way up it, dismounted and led his horse the rest of the way, stopped on the near-side when his eyes were able to rake the downhill country on the far side. Stood there watching for movement for a long time, then, when he saw it far ahead but not as far as he privately thought he'd have been if he'd been running from someone, he mounted again, descended the hill and watched his back-trail. There was no movement down there but the trees obscured most of that end of the world.

Making no attempt to track the boy any more, he selected the best route for his horse and pushed the animal hard for two sweaty hours. By then he could see the big horse with its thin, undersized rider every now and then and kept the livery animal at a hurrying walk until he was close enough for his final strategy. He made no attempt to approach the boy from the rear. Treated him exactly as though he were a desperate outlaw. Circled wide around him and waited on the same game-trail Carter was using. Stood beside his horse listening to the approaching rider, almost with a smile in his dark eyes.

When the last switch-back in the trail separated them — Mark always took advantage of switch-backs; they would meet head-on at less than ten feet when they finally met and every advantage would lie with him — he could hear Carter talking to the horse, telling him the things that had been bottled up in a little boy's heart for a long time. Then they were facing one another. The boy's horse snorted in surprise. Carter's mouth fell open, his eyes flew wide open.

"Howdy, Cart." He made it gentle, almost jocular, but his eyes never left the hands two feet in front of the bulging shirt-front. "I had to do some figuring to catch up with you."

The thin face was white, the eyes dry looking. There was a purple bruise down across the boy's left cheek. It ended in a sullen-looking break on the chin. Anger rose slowly, snow-balling, deep inside Mark. Quirt mark. He hid the anger — he hoped — in the first smile he'd shown in a long time.

"Climb down. Let's see what you've got in your sack. I'm hungry enough to eat a Comanche."

The boy's stiffness left him all at once. He seemed to buckle in the middle, sag all over at once. A darting tongue went lightning-like around his lips and disappeared.

"Were you — hunting me?"

"Naw," Mark said, seeing where the blood had been wiped from the chin, seeing the stain of shed tears through the grime of the white, pinched face. "I just came after you is all. How're you going to get that Comanche lance if you aren't around when it gets here?" He smiled wider with a lump the size of an egg in his throat. God damn a man who'd use a quirt on a kid that size. "How about it — would you share your poke with a hungry man?"

Carter groped with one hand for the little sack he had tied to his waist. He was bareback. The big horse he was riding was a good animal, strong and powerful looking. Irrevelantly Mark thought it was a good thing he hadn't had to chase the lad. His livery horse never would have caught the big bay.

Carter slid down, still watching Mark uncertainly, holding his reins and feeling for the food-sack knot without looking around. "You're going to take me back, aren't you?"

Mark shook his head and the smile died. "I didn't plan to, Cart. Now I know I won't."

The sack came loose and the boy held it out. "Here," he said, "the cornbread's all crumbled but the meat's good. It's bear meat."

Mark took the sack and squatted, opened it and poked a hand inside. The food, obviously hastily taken, was jumbled, covered with lint from the sack and almost unrecognisable. He tore off a piece of meat and chewed it.

"Sit down, Cart. You're hungry too, aren't you?"

"No." The boy sat, watching Mark's thick arms, his whisker-stubbled face, his jaws ripple as he chewed, and his dark eyes.

"You got to eat though. A man can't travel on grit alone. Come on." He held out the sack. "The meat's good."

Carter took the sack, peered into it. His blond hair was tumbled. There were pine needles in it, and dirt. He'd slept on the ground. There was no blanket and it'd been pretty cool at dawn.

"Where's your bed-roll, Cart? A man can't get much rest all doubled up like a 'coon, these nights."

"I don't have one." The boy looked interestedly at a cornbread-speckled piece of meat with lint enough on it to look like it had a fur coating. Very solemnly he began to pick the lint off.

"Where were you going?"

"Away. Out to California."

"Oh," Mark said gravely. "Awful long way."

The blue eyes came up. A little colour had leaked back into the boy's face. "Why did you follow me, Mark? Because I stoled the horse?"

Mark swallowed and found it a little difficult. "The horse doesn't mean a hill of beans to me, Cart," he said. "I always figure a good man shouldn't run from anything because somewhere there's someone who'll sort of — well — help 'im, maybe."

"Help me?" Carter said. He raised a filthy hand to the bruise. "See this?"

"Yes, I see it. Why'd he give it to you?"

"Oh — it was my fault. I said something about the Comanch' spear. I didn't mean to, it just slipped out."

"Yeah," Mark said. "And he got the rest of it out of you. About me talking to you."

"Yes. Boy! I've never seen him that mad before." The boy's fingers fluttered at his shirt buttons. "Look," he said.

Mark looked at the thin chest, the curling strips of peeled flesh across the shoulders and looked away with murder in his heart. He didn't trust himself to say anything so he didn't. Carter buttoned the shirt up and shoved the sack at him.

"Eat some more."

"Can't do it, Cart. I'm full up."

The boy looked from Mark's face into the little sack and said, "It's sort of jumbled up, isn't it?"

142

Mark stood up swiftly and rubbed hard at one cheek. The whisker stubble made a rasping, grating sound. "I never tasted anything better, and that's a fact, but eating heavy when you're riding's poor business." He made a cigarette, lit it and considered the time elapse. Wondered just how far back Erastus Diamond was. There was something else in the back of his mind. It had come suddenly, almost breathtakingly, into his consciousness. He stood now, examining it, considering it gingerly.

Carter got up and tied the sack very carefully to his belt. "Mark? How'd you come down from in front of me?"

The dark eyes dropped. "I circled around you, Cart. See, it's like this. Never come up on a man you're chasing from behind. If he thinks you might be behind him he can ambush you, but if you pick a spot up ahead of him where he'll be too close to use a gun when you come onto him, you've got more of a break than he has. He's not expecting you up front. If he's watchin' at all, he's watchin' his back-trail."

"Oh," Carter said musingly. "Yeah — sure. That's pretty smart, isn't it?" He fingered the sack at his waist. "What are you going to do now?"

Mark heard the anxiety, saw it in the boy's

eyes. "We're going to sit around here in the shade for a while."

"Here?" Carter said, mystified.

"Yeah. Your paw'll be along in a little while."

"My paw?" A rush of fear flooded the boy's eyes.

"Yeah; we're going to have a three-way talk. You and me and him. Y'see, Cart, I don't like that quirting business. Tell me something; did you ever quirt a dog or a horse until he was bleeding?"

"No."

"Would you?"

"No. I'm chicken-livered, maw says."

Mark nodded absently. "Me too. I'm pretty chicken-livered too. We'll talk a little with your paw."

"Are you going to — bushwhack him?"

Mark was startled. "Bushwhack him? Lord no, boy. That's no way for a man to do."

"Then what are you going to do?" The blue eyes were still, wide and perplexed. "You're a lot bigger'n him, Mark."

Mark nodded again. "I'm not going to touch him, Cart. Not unless he makes me do it. I don't think he will though. You think he's all right, don't you?"

The answer was low and reluctantly said. "Not any more, I don't. I tried to. My real

144

paw wouldn't have done that, I bet."

Mark's attention, divided, half-listening to the silence around them, closed down around the boy's words. "Your real paw? Well — isn't Erastus Diamond your real paw?"

Cart shook his head. "Oh no. My real paw's dead. He died with the pox a long time ago."

"Oh." Mark was silent a while, then he said, "Where's your Mother?"

"She died when I was born. My paw told me that."

"Well . . . Don't you have any kinfolks, Cart?"

"No. I don't know any. My paw said we had some back in Indiana somewhere, but he never did tell me much about them."

Mark's knees felt rubbery. He knelt and studied the distant rise and fall of countryside without seeing it at all. Finally he said, "Cart — I got a proposition to make you. You know, this isn't right, really, but maybe if it works out right — well — maybe then it'd be right." The boy was regarding him uncomprehendingly and he hurried on. "I've been thinking. Y'see, Cart — I had a son about your age. He — died. Well, now, I've been thinking. What d'you think of me buying you from Mister Diamond," the dark eyes wavered, steadied up and stayed on

145

Carter's face. "And make you *my* kid instead of his? What do you think about that?"

Carter's mouth dropped open then snapped closed. The boy's eyes warmed very suddenly, colour suffused his cheeks and he looked away. For a while there was just the silence of the brooding land, then he said, "What if he wouldn't sell me? Anyway — "

"We can fix that when he gets up here, Cart. Uh — would you like that, you reckon?"

The boy's profile showed where he swallowed twice and he didn't look at Mark when he answered. "Golly, Mark. I'd . . ." An unshed tear trembled on the brink of an eyelid. "Golly — I sure would!"

Mark snuffed out his cigarette, avoided looking at the trembling mouth, the shoulders trying so hard not to quake, and got to his feet, cleared his throat and held out the reins to the livery horse. "All right, Cart, we'll try it. Now then — you take your horse and my horse down a trail a ways." He looked around. "Down about where that creek is, and wait with 'em down there. Let 'em graze. They're hungry by now."

Carter still looked away when he felt for the reins. Mark saw the bulge under the shirt-front again. "And say, Cart — do me

146

a favour, will you?"

"Sure."

"Don't touch that gun you're wearing no matter what happens. Promise?"

"Promise."

He let the reins slide through his fingers and then, briefly, very swiftly and lightly, he touched the boy's awry hair. "Just like pardners, Cart. Let 'em graze and don't do anything until I call you."

"Sure, Mark."

The horses passed by obediently, sniffing one another out of curiosity and Mark didn't turn to look after them until the sound of their passage faded out, then he drew in a big breath, expelled it and watched the sunlight flash dully off Carter's head as he walked head-down, ahead of the animals. A strange peacefulness was in him, almost an exaltation. When a man loses a lot, he thought, maybe he's supposed to get back a little. Maybe bitterness normally blinds him to what otherwise he'd see. It could have happened here, if he had just concentrated on Diamond and Timmons.

He took his stance in the trail, wide-legged, warm under the curling heat that was filtered through some scraggly, ancient trees nearby, and told himself he was learning something in this Cascade country. He was learning a lot. Most of it had to do with himself, too. In way, sort of, some of it seemed to echo a little of what Eileen had said over the years. Not just Eileen, but Jonathon Buell too.

Buell . . . He'd acted strange when Mark had come back to Cascade from Bordenton on the trail of Darrel Timmons. Had acted as though he were hiding something, or maybe it was like he'd said. Maybe he didn't *want* Mark to find Timmons because he was afraid Mark would kill the outlaw. Well, he meant to kill him and he still meant to kill him — whichever of the two caused Will's death, and if they were both responsible, he meant to kill them both. Buell had acted oddly though and in the back of his mind while he waited for Ras Diamond to come, something close to uneasiness kept prodding him.

Buell was no fool. He'd thought so at first but now he knew a sight better. Buell had a knack of reading signs that he didn't pick up off the ground, the way Mark'd been Texas-trained to do.

He moved deeper into the shade of the trail. Threw back his head and gazed at the sun. It was getting close to the meridian.

Maybe he shouldn't do anything about Timmons until after he'd talked it all over

148

again with Jonathon. Diamond would tell him what he wanted to know, specifically. He'd get that if he had to beat it out of Diamond. And there was the matter of quirting Carter; Diamond'd settle for that too. But before he went after Timmons, regardless of what Diamond said — and he could almost guess what that would be; he'd cornered enough outlaws to know they all laid the blame on whichever one of their cronies were absent — regardless of that, he'd stop in Cascade and talk to Jonathon again.

The necessity grew in his mind as the moments flicked by. Something he couldn't fathom urged him to do it. He promised himself he'd see Jonathon as soon as he could.

And Carter. What would Eileen say? What would Jonathon say? Perhaps he'd been hasty. No, not hasty. Hell's bells, you couldn't let a man like Diamond take him back and you couldn't just wish him well and watch him ride off into the sunset, beyond which — a thousand miles! — lay California.

But the thought of Eileen's reaction bothered him deeply and unstintingly. He worried over it, crossed his big arms over his chest and assembled arguments in favour of what he had done. What he would do, when Diamond came along. The result was a stubbornness that grew in him that no matter what:

if Eileen turned away from the little boy, Mark would still see that he had his chance because every boy deserved a chance. Needed if not a father, then a sort of step-pardner, to steer him right. Stand behind him, back him up.

Step-pardner.

The name hung up in his mind, gathered substance when he said it aloud. Acquired a meaning that seemed to Mark to have more depth, more sincere meaning than step-father. He liked it and it made him feel warm, thinking of it.

What brought his mind away from the designation was the cry of a flashy magpie that went hurtling past, excited. He uncrossed his arms, flexed them, worked his fingers and moved out of the shadows, back into the trail just around the switch-back.

Moments later he heard the horse coming. The sound of shod hooves, the swish of brush when a man hunched his shoulders, twisted through it. A glance down where Cart and the horses were showed him the boy sitting in the shade with his feet in the creek, his head low on his shoulders. The horses grazing close to him.

He turned back again, waiting . . .

Chapter Six

If Erastus Diamond had been a brave man, even a recklessly brave man, it is unlikely that he would have gone for his gun when he came plodding around the switch-back in the trail, bent far out of his saddle, frowning in concentration at two sets of horse tracks where he had reason to expect only one. The reason Ras never had a chance was exactly that. He was bent over so far he was off-balance and when his horse flung back, stiff-legged from the big man standing there in the trail, Ras had to fight for his balance. He never had a chance to reach for the pistol on his hip or the carbine-butt jutting upwards from the saddleboot.

Straightening, Ras saw Mark. Saw his easy stance, his swept-back right arm fingers inches above the hand-gun at his side. He was frightened and astonished at the same time. He made no move to interfere when Mark moved closer, lifted his gun and threw it aside, took one rein from Ras's hand and stood off to one side, gazing up at him.

"Get down, Diamond."

Ras dismounted awkwardly, still shocked, still speechless with astonishment. His pinched features, their vicious mouth slack, looked mottled and unclean.

"You can guess what I want from you, Diamond."

Ras's faded eyes hung to Mark's face, unblinking, looking like oak-smoke on a wintry, overcast sky. "What," he said. "What d'you want of me — now?"

"Where did you and Timmons bury the money off those stages? Where is Timmons?"

Ras's jaws worked, his face was pallid. "I ain't seen Timmons in a 'coon's age."

Diamond's horse, the same spooky one that'd been in the little corral back at the cabin, threw up its head, scenting the horses down by the creek. Mark looped the reins around the horn and waved his arm, the animal trotted, head high, tail straight out, down the trail toward Carter, his bay and Mark's livery beast.

Mark rolled his head a little to one side. He sounded very matter-of-fact, very deliberate, when he spoke. "Diamond, you're a liar. You know plenty about Darrel Timmons and I'm going to make you a bet. You're going to tell me all you know. Every blessed word of it. Want to bet?"

"You're jus' talkin', Mister. In the first place I don't know Timmons hardly at all. In the second place I got my rights. You nor anyone else can go riding aroun' — "

"Shut up! That's better. Now let me tell you something, Diamond. I know who Timmons is. I know who you are. I know the two o' you work that stage robbing game. You use Rafferty's horses. You plan it good and up until now you've made it stick. Now, this'll be the last time I ask you. *Where is Timmons?*"

"I hones'-to-gawd don't know where he's went."

"When did you see him last."

"Today," Ras said roughly. "He come by this morning."

He knows I know that, Mark thought. He got that much out of Cart. Aloud he said: "What did he want, when he came by?"

"Wanted to sell me his sorrel horse."

Mark moved in a little closer. His face was perfectly expressionless, like his eyes. Dangerously still, blank looking. "You're lying again, Diamond." His hand flashed up and the sound broke into dozens of tiny echoes. Diamond's head rolled weakly on his shoulders. He threw out a hand as though to steady himself.

"What did you talk about, Diamond?"

"That damned horse of his. And . . . ."

"And?" The dark eyes flickered, the hand half-raised.

"Movin' on; gettin' out of this damned country."

Mark hooked one thumb in his shell-belt. "Going to take your money and leave?"

"What money you talkin' about?"

Mark's big arm rose, hovered and fell with the weight of a small tree. His fingers curled around Diamond's shirt, closed down harder and drew the lesser man up close. So close their faces were inches apart.

"The money you got from the stage hold-ups, Diamond. The money you got by stealing Rafferty's horses, riding out and robbing stages." His voice cracked, the echoes sharp-edged, fierce.

Diamond made a weak, contorting movement with his body. "I'm a sick man," he said.

Mark flung him away. "Where did you two hide that money? Don't lie because I'm going to get it out of you if I have to break you in two to do it."

"I don't have any money."

"Where is it?"

The sun shone off the dull sweat on Diamond's face. He looked pale, looked actually unwell. The corners of his mouth were moist, his eyes moved ceaselessly. "Darrel's got it." The words were so low Mark wasn't sure he'd heard right.

"What?"

"He's got it — Timmons. He took it this mornin' when he come back from Bordenton. He said the law was nosin' around. Then — when th' damned kid — "

"That's all I want to know right now," Mark said flatly. "Save the rest of it. You and Timmons worked it between you — I mean, how to steal Rafferty's horses then turn them loose. Why?"

"Make it look like someone from town was doin' it."

"I believe that," Mark said. He stood a moment in silence studying Diamond. "Which one of you killed the boy who was with Rafferty's horses?"

Diamond's face underwent a shocked, appalled, and complete change. "Killed th' kid? We didn't kill no kid."

"You damned liar!"

"Hones' to gawd! The kid shot at us, but we had the horses on the run by then. Didn't neither o' us shoot back. That's gospel truth, Mister. Gospel truth."

It was possible that Timmons had done it without Diamond knowing it. Mark didn't believe, after witnessing Diamond's astonishment, that Diamond had done it. He wasn't intelligent enough to be that good an actor. So it was Timmons; at least he'd withhold judgement until he could put them together and ask the question again.

He didn't believe that Will had shot at the thieves. Buell had told him the old gun had no firing-pin. That was a detail. What stuck in his mind was Diamond's look; whatever *had* happened, Diamond wasn't clear about it. He'd put them together. He'd also query Jonathon. The constable, he thought, was looming large in this. His decision only confirmed the earlier one: wait and talk to Jonathon.

"One more thing, Diamond. Your kid, Carter; you've got no right to him."

"*I* didn't want him, my old lady did. Wanted him to fetch and haul around the place. He's a no-good lit— "

"Shut up! Diamond, I'm going to let you set a price on what he's cost you. I'm going to pay you what you think it's cost you and take him myself."

The watery eyes widened. "Pay f'him? You mean — like buyin' a horse?"

"Call it that if you want. Give it any name under the sun but from right now on, Cart's my kid not yours."

"Why — b'God — you're welcome to

him. Take him and well shed I call it. Damned little — "

"Cart?" Mark called loudly. "Oh, Cart!"

"Yes? I'm coming."

Mark turned to Diamond with his lips drawn back. "Don't get abusive, Diamond. Not in front of him. I'll back-hand you silly the first crack you make."

Carter came up and his eyes were shuntling between them, afraid, like the eyes of a trapped animal. "Yes, Mark?"

"Mister Diamond's just agreed you can come with me from now on." He looked over at the smaller, wirier man. "Tell him, Diamond."

Diamond looked at the boy with veiled hate showing in spite of him. "You heard what he said. You're his'n from now." He raised his head and gazed stonily at Mark, saying nothing.

Mark could feel the closeness of the boy, his breath on the back of his hand. Without looking down at him he said, "You can bring up our horses, Cart. We'll head back now."

When Carter trotted away Mark looked at Ras Diamond a long time in silence, then he said, "That was a good quirting job you did on him. I'm going to remember that. If it takes me ten years, Diamond, I'm going

157

to make you wish a hundred times you never did that."

The outlaw kept his mouth closed. He waited, slouch-shouldered, until the animals were brought up.

Mark used his lariat to make a lead-rope to the leggy bay horse Carter had ridden. He tied a bowline and ran the rope down through the curb-strap and up to the saddle-horn of the horse Diamond had ridden. "Here y'are, Cart. You lead us. Keep the rope fast to your horn. If he tries to bust past you just set your dallies and leave the rest to me. I can wing him before he gets fifty feet. All ready; get up there then."

"But — this is *his* horse, Mark."

"I know, pardner, only *he's* going to ride bareback from here on, you aren't." He waited until the boy had the reins gathered up, the dallies snugged up around the horn, then he turned and motioned for Erastus Diamond to mount the leggy bay without any saddle. Diamond screwed up his face, grabbed the hand-holt of hair where the beast's mane began at the withers, and with a loud grunt, a spring, landed astride. Mark mounted the livery horse and grinned at Cart.

"Lead him out, Cart, and don't worry, I'll be right behind him. His first mistake'll be his last."

They rode back over the twisting game trail, bucked their way through brush and crossed dappled glens of shade where the trees interrupted the afternoon sunshine. Rode steadily without a stop or a word for a long time, and at last Carter reined up and pointed where the Diamond cabin, its rubble-strewn yard drearily blightful in the waning light, lay.

Mark said, "Bear to your right, Cart. Go 'way out and around it. Through the trees." He kneed up beside Diamond. The two men looked at one another and Mark's thin smile was humorless. "You could call out, Diamond." The way he said it made the outlaw turn his head away, look straight ahead with a fierce cant to his jaw.

When they broke into the clearing near the Diamond ranch cut-off Cart was raising his rein-hand again when Mark said, "South, Cart. South until you hit the stage road, then follow it into Cascade."

The evening shadows came slowly, unpretentiously. The sun became a huge red disc that coloured the world in diluted blood, broke over the land and drenched it, traded heat for vividness so that distance shrank and every tree they passed, every grass-smothered outcropping of lichened rock, was stark. It was still hot but the heat dwindled as they came into the stage road and went down it. A spindrift of powder-fine dust arose, not much, just a little. Enough to gather like silk in the feathers around their horses' fetlocks.

Cascade came up to them as Mark had seen it before. With the sun-shadows hard, slantingly, across the lower portions of the buildings and the blood-red higher, up along the false-fronts, splashed across the perpendicular signs, and with the evening sounds of people and animals muted, as though each and all were unconsciously hushed, offering instinctive homage to the twilight's coolness.

"Head for the liverybarn, Cart."

Rafferty was lighting a cigar when they rode up. He had a bowler on the back of his head. His day was done. Looking over the cupped edges of his hands he let the match die. His eyes caught them one by one, Cart first, then Erastus Diamond, finally Mark. The shrewd coldness wavered, slid away. A wondering watchfulness took its place. Rafferty struck another match, drew on the cigar, snapped the matchstick and dropped it, exhaled fragrant smoke and didn't move. Supper could wait, he wanted to see this.

Carter was craning his head, looking at Mark who dismounted and winked very solemnly at the boy. "All right, Cart. From now on he's mine. You did a good job." With an infinitesimal jerk of his head to Diamond he said, "Get down."

Rafferty rolled the cigar in his lips, went over where the shade was and watched. So he'd gotten Ras Diamond; well, everyone expected he'd get someone, only Cascade had laid its wagers he'd bring his man in tied across a horse, leaking blood.

"To Buell's office, Diamond."

Carter walked beside Mark, his eyes filled with a strange and glowing light. People stood and stared. A ripple went through the town. Men ducked into doorways, spoke, and others tumbled out to see.

Jonathon was standing with his back to them when they came up. He was bent over muttering at the lock, which for some reason didn't want to snap this one night.

"Jonathon."

The constable turned, lock dangling from his fingers. His eyebrows were raised in mechanical, interrogative patience. They dropped, settled into a tufted, grey line as straight as the mouth of a bear-trap. He closed his fist over the lock.

"Well, well. Hello Ras. Hello son, glad to see the three of you upright." A thumb jerked sideways. "Come on in."

Mark prodded Ras. Carter trailed behind Mark with his breath coming short. Mark pushed Diamond onto the little bench and stood by the door. Jonathon fumbled in an untidy desk drawer until he came up with a horseshoe bent closed, forming a circle from which hung several large, forbidding looking keys. He went toward the cell-room door and beckoned to Ras Diamond.

"Come on, Ras."

When the sound of their voices, their footfalls, died away, Carter took over Diamond's vacated bench and grinned uncertainly up at Mark. "Want some of our grub?" he asked.

Mark thought how the bear meat and cornbread must look by now and sat down on an edge of Jonathon's desk. "We'll go buy us a cafe supper directly, Cart, but if you're starving go right ahead. 'Believe I'll just wait."

"Me, too," Carter said quickly. "I just thought you might be hungry."

"I am. Tell you what. Why don't you go across the road to the cafe and get good and washed up and order us both a big dinner. That way I won't have to wait when I'm through here." He fished out some cartwheels — big, silver dollars — and handed them to Cart. "And if you wanted to, you could buy a clean shirt and maybe a new

162

pair of breeches." He stopped speaking, dug deeper with a recklessness he hadn't felt in a long time and put more cartwheels in the lad's hand. "And a pair of boots. They've got 'em at the emporium that have genuine copper toe-plates on 'em. All right?"

Carter didn't answer, he just nodded and the swimming look was back in his eyes. Mark got off the desk and went over by the stove with his back to the boy. "But you'd better hurry because the stores'll close on you. I'll be over in a few minutes."

Carter left and Jonathon Buell came back into the room with a questioning look on his face. "Well," he said, "what happened? How'd you come to fetch *him* in?"

Mark told him how he'd eavesdropped, trailed Carter and waited for Ras Diamond and brought him back. He also told him what Ras had said about the robberies.

Jonathon flung the keys on his desk carelessly and sank down into his chair. "Something happened while you were gone, Mark. A man got killed on the stage road. A dispatch rider. Killed and robbed. It happened last night. I guess it must've happened before you got up there in the back-country by Diamond's place."

Mark was frowning. "Not another holdup," he said dully. "This is a hell of a country."

163

"I don't think so," Jonathon said, unperturbed. "But this one's got me stumped for sure." He settled deeper into his chair. "Some folks found him about midnight. I went up, me and the doc in a wagon, and brought him back." Buell's eyes flicked over Mark's face. "Now, here's the cussed part about this. This here feller wasn't shot, he was clubbed from one side, but he must've had a pretty thick brain-box because there's sign around up there of him putting up quite a scrap before he keeled over. He never got at his gun but he had a Bowie knife and he laid it about plenty from the looks of the ground."

Mark made a weary gesture with his hand. "That one's yours, oldtimer. This one's my last. As soon's I've got Darrel Timmons I'm dropping out for good."

"I don't blame you," Jonathon said in the same unperturbed way. "You've got a reason. What'd you do with the boy?"

"Sent him across to the cafe to order us some dinner. Jonathon, I want to ask you something. How's Eileen?"

"She's about the same, I'd say, Mark." He wagged his head. "It'll take a long time, son, a long time. It isn't just the boy, it's you and a lot of other things."

"Yes, I know. Jonathon — I took Carter

away from Diamond. He said he was glad to get shed of him."

"I suppose he was, the way he looked at the boy."

"Jonathon — I want Eileen to see him. I want her to like him so we can keep him."

"You can't trade one for the other, Mark."

"No, I'm not trying to, only he's had a sort of a bad time and — "

"I understand. Diamond give him that quirt mark across the face?"

"You ought to see his chest and shoulders."

Jonathon said nothing. His nostrils pinched down against expelled breath.

"Do you see, Jonathon?"

"Sure. Fact is, I — well — I wasn't exactly surprised it came out like this. Not really. I had a hunch about you and young Carter. Y'know, I knew his pappy before he passed on. He was a nice feller, quiet and easy-going. Smart, too, but somewhere along the line he'd come loose at the seams. I always thought it was the dead wife that did it to him. He just didn't have the will to live, Mark, and when he got the pox he died. Lost his will to live, to find happiness, somewhere along the route; see?"

"I see. What was his name? His last name?"

"Cussed if I know. Everybody called him

165

Soapy. That's all any of us knew. The kid don't know because I asked him when his paw died. He was a lot younger then, maybe five, six years old, maybe younger. He just knew his father as paw. Hell, he might've been an outlaw for all I know. Me and the rest of Cascade."

"It doesn't matter, does it?" Mark said.

"Not a damned bit, Mark. Not a damned bit. Y'know, I used to think about taking Cart in myself, but I'm too old. A feller like him needs a — "

"A step-pardner," Mark interrupted.

Jonathon's eyes kindled and he nodded. "Well — that fits it like a boot. He needs a step-pardner. Feller your age. Eileen's age."

"What do you think, Jonathon?"

The constable screwed up his face and leaned forward, eyes closed, and put his head into cupped hands. "I hope, Mark. I just hope to God. You've got to do the talking to her, I can't or I would. It's up to you, boy."

Mark sat morosely for a while longer, then he shook himself inwardly. "I'll see," he said. "How is Eileen?"

"Well, about all I can say is that you've got to talk to her, Mark. Got to bring her out of it."

"Out of what, the grief?"

"Yes, that," Jonathon said, "but there's something else too. I don't exactly know how to describe it. She's sort of sinking. Sets all days and doesn't eat or talk or nothing. It's got my wife worried sick. We think if anyone can do it you can. You've got to try."

Mark got up. "I will, Jonathon. I'll try right after supper." He went across the road to the cafe. The sight of Carter was warming. His face shone almost as brightly as his eyes did. He had a stiff-new pair of pants, a blue shirt that matched his eyes and his stiff, thick hair was weighted down with water, but in back some stubbornly rebellious strands stood straight up. When Mark crossed the room Carter pushed his feet around the edge of the table. New boots with copper toe-plates shone with a proudness that equalled the boy's own pride in them. Mark sat down and smiled.

"Sure are pretty, Cart."

"I've got some money left too."

"Enough to pay for supper?"

"Yes, and a little more."

"All right," Mark said, "you can treat me to a supper then we'll go calling."

The food came. Mark ate but Carter touched his food without showing much interest in it. "Where, Mark?"

"Over to the constable's house, Cart. My wife's staying over there."

"Oh." Carter's eyes fell to the plate with a shadow of uneasiness in them. "We got to?"

Mark looked over at him. "Well — it's not to see the constable," he said. "It's to visit a little. Social call is all. Anyway, you'll like the folks there." Under his breath and to himself he said "I hope" and went on eating. When they were finished Mark felt much better.

They went out into the evening. The air was rich and soft and as clear as glass. A piano was making sad music in one of the saloons. Not fast music nor jangling music, sad music. Mark made a cigarette with the strains running through his head, touching out along his nerves. The music affected him in a way he couldn't have defined, explained. He lit the cigarette letting the sensation of bitter sweetness have its way with him.

Across the road and down a ways Jonathon's office showed a liquid flow of gold lamp-light. Four horses were standing head-down at the rack before the office's overhang. Two men were slouching near the door. One was smoking the other was just leaning against the wall, thumbs hooked in his shell-belt, one leg cocked up behind, on the wall.

Mark looked and wondered a little and a pin-prick of suspicion touched him. He smoked thoughtfully. Around him flowed the town's night-life; people strolling in the coolness, talking, meeting here and there in the soft gloom, laughing now and then. Carter reached up and touched his arm. He looked around and down. The boy's face was white and tired looking in the shadows.

"We goin' down there now?"

Mark looked back toward the constable's office and hesitated over his answer. "In a little while, Cart. Come on, let's go see what's going on over at Mister Buell's."

They crossed the roadway, the big, massive man and the wisp of a boy, stepped up onto the far sidewalk and went south a few doors. Carter's new boots made a solid sound on the hollow boards, the copper toe-plates shone in a dull way; with absorbed rapture, their owner watched them move.

One of the men at the door of the constable's office straightened up when Mark and Carter swung in. The whites of his eyes showed in the deeper shadow under his hatbrim. Mark gave him look for look and pressed against the door, it gave. He and Carter entered.

There were two men in the room with

Jonathon. There also was an atmosphere of electrical discord. Jonathon was facing the two men from behind his desk, his face relaxed but stubborn looking. When Mark and Carter entered he turned slightly, looked at them both, and smiled in a wintry way.

"Howdy Carter. Glad y'stopped by, Mark. These fellers are from the ranches. They got a complaint. They say the law's not doing enough about these robberies and now this killin' on the stage road. They want us to stop those things."

Mark looked at the two strangers. They were cowmen by their dress and looks. Uncompromising men, too. There was no welcome in either set of eyes. In a rattling dry tone of voice Mark said, "Have they any suggestions or just complaints?"

One of the men, older, as lean as a rail, snapped an answer. "We got a suggestion. A younger constable."

Mark looked at the man. "Well," he said, "that might be a solution, but I don't think it would. Catching outlaws isn't as simple as you fellers seem to think."

"No?" the other rancher said sourly. "Where I come from we caught 'em without too much trouble."

"Is that so? Where did you come from?"

"Texas," the cowman said, exclaiming the

170

name like it was a banner.

Mark's dark eyes grew sardonic. "I came from Texas too, Mister. I learnt lawing under the Rangers down there. Since I've been up here I've learnt a lot more about lawing. In Texas we used to make up a posse and go hell-for-leather over the range until we ran a man down. After that we prosecuted him. It usually worked, too, but since I've been up here I've sort of wondered just how many innocent men we railroaded into prison. I've got where I don't think too much about that kind of law any more."

"It cleaned out the rattlesnakes," the cowman said.

"It made outlaws scarce all right, but I think it's better to go slower and make sure, now."

The older man broke in with an impatient, waspish toss of his head. "Who're you, anyway?"

"My name's Mark Carter. I've been working with Jonathon for a few days."

The man's face underwent a swift change. "Carter?" he said, and words lay in his eyes; questions.

"Yeh, Carter." Mark could see the questions. He nodded. "That's right. That was my boy."

The cowmen fell back into silence, looking

at him. They stood in discomfort until the older one looked around at Jonathon again. "Well, Jonathon, just wanted you to know how folks in the country feel. Especially about the lad."

"I know," Jonathon said quietly. "I feel the same way maybe even more so. We're doing everything we can."

"How long'll it take, Jonathon? Folks're roiled up."

"Not much longer," Jonathon said. "A couple of days maybe. Maybe not that long. Listen, Jeff, everything that can be done is being done. You know that. You've known me too many years to think I'm not doing my job. As far as age is concerned — Jeff, an old lawdog's better'n a young one any time. I know what I'm talking about."

The ranchers exchanged a glance then the older man nodded. "All right. We'll let it ride for a day or so." He nodded to Mark and went out followed by the younger man.

Mark gazed at Jonathon. "What roused them up all of a sudden?"

"Will, mostly, then the robberies, and now this man that got beat t'death up on the road. You can't blame 'em, Mark." Jonathon stooped, rummaged in his desk drawer and brought out a battered old six-gun which he held out towards Mark. "Will's," he said.

Mark took the gun, looked down at it, cocked it and stood perfectly still, almost holding his breath, for the hammer, drawn back, showed a very sharp and jutting firing-pin. After a long moment he raised his eyes to Jonathon's face. "You said it had no firing-pin, Jonathon."

"It didn't have, Mark. When I give him that old gun the pin was plumb out of it."

Mark looked down at the gun again. Was still staring at the firing-pin when Jonathon fished out something from his shirt pocket, held it out toward Mark. It was an extra hammer to a Colt's .44. The firing-pin on the old hammer was filed off.

Mark looked at the hammer in Jonathon's palm and understood. His son had managed to get hold of another hammer for his crippled gun. He had installed the good one so the gun would shoot.

"Where did you find that, Jonathon?"

"Among his treasures at the shack."

"Oh." Mark handed the gun back to the constable. "Keep this for me, Jonathon, I want it, but not right now." Jonathon put the old gun back in his desk and stood there looking at Mark. The younger man's eyes were on the floor. "Then he *did* shoot at them."

Jonathon still said nothing. There was a

strange, almost pleading look in his face.

"Getting bullets wouldn't be hard, would it?"

"No."

Mark rocked back and forth gently on the balls of his feet then he let out a long sigh and looked up. "I guess I'll go see Eileen, Jonathon."

"Fine," the constable said. "Leave Cart here with me."

Mark's glance clouded. He paused over a reply. "I'd figured on taking him with me."

Jonathon shook his head very gently, very slightly. "Not right now, Mark. Maybe afterwards but not right this minute."

A wisp of the older man's wisdom brushed lightly across Mark's consciousness. He looked down at the boy. "Will you stay here a little while, Cart?"

"Sure, Mark."

The big Texan put a hand on one thin shoulder and squeezed gently. "Thanks, pardner. Mister Buell an' you ought to get to know one another anyway, I reckon." Still with his hand on Carter's shoulder he looked up at Jonathon. "All right," he said. "S'long."

Carter watched Mark leave, felt the silence in the office, the depressing environment he was surrounded with and avoided looking at Constable Buell. Jonathon was a little at a loss himself, then he sat down and motioned Carter toward the little wooden bench.

"Sit down, Cart. We can visit until he gets back."

Mark crossed the road and turned south until he came to the end of the square, then turned left and trod the uneven, nearly dry lumpiness of the road as far as the picket-fence. There, the old dog came snuffling, alternately growling and whining. He went through the gate and up to the door, the dog ambling along behind him in a groping way. Lamp-light cast its yellow softness over the worn and aged front of the house, struck the big man standing there with his hat in one hand, the other hand raised to knock on the door.

Jonathon's wife admitted him. Beyond her, past her plump shoulder he saw Eileen sitting in a dark red chair with antimacassars on the arms and where one's head would rest. The dark profusion of her hair, glowing like charcoal with dew on it, backgrounded the paleness of her face, the dullness of her eyes which lifted to his face. Jonathon's wife left the room. A big wooden-cased clock with scroll-like hands lent its soft, measured beat to the silence. He crossed to her and stooped, put both large hands on the white doilies on the chair.

"Eileen — I want you to take a little walk with me."

The dull eyes stayed on his face, dry looking, with no shine of inner life showing in them. She said, "Did you find them, Mark?"

"No. I mean, I don't want to talk about that. Take a walk with me."

"Why?"

He pushed off the chair, held one of her cold hands. "I want to talk. It comes easier outside." He pulled gently, she didn't resist but she didn't stand up either, just leaned forward with the tug on her hand.

"About the funeral," she said. "Tomorrow morning."

It wasn't relevant. He looked closer at her, saw the peculiar blankness in her eyes and stopped exerting pressure on her hand, held it still but with a perfectly motionless, dawning uneasiness. He was facing something that was far beyond him. He placed her hand back in her lap and turned away, went through the house until he found Jonathon's wife in the kitchen and faced her.

"Is she sick? I — could a doctor help her?"

The older woman, slight but sturdy facing his bigness, shook her head in grey-eyed thoughtfulness. "A doctor can't help her,

Mister Carter, but she's ill. It's a sickness of the spirit, not just the heart. It's a terrible thing. The boy — of course — but it's something else too."

He looked down at the immaculate table his hand was resting upon. "Is it me?"

"You, yes. You and the boy and something else I'd say was a hopelessness. She's lost too many things all at once. She's numbed by her losses. Stricken by them."

He looked up. "I want to take her for a walk in the dark. I want to talk to her but I feel like what I say doesn't reach her some-how."

Mrs. Buell regarded his ruddy face, the dark eyes with their moving background of bewilderment. She nodded up at him. "I think you should make her go for a walk. She just sits and stares. I think she's got to be shaken out of herself. I can't do it but you might be able to." Almost fiercely she said, "I wish the funeral was over. I wish this was a year from now." She coloured a little and brushed at a stray wisp of hair with the back of one hand and changed the subject. "When will Jonathon be home?"

"Jonathon? Oh, directly, I reckon. I left him at the office with Carter Diamond. He's minding him until I come back."

"Carter Diamond?" Her glance brightened.

"Did Jonathon fetch him down here to town?"

"No, I brought him back with me. That's one of the things I want to talk to my wife about."

"Yes," Mrs. Buell said vigorously. "Well now, I'll get her wrap and you make her go for a walk with you." Her grey eyes jumped to his face again. "It's warm out isn't it?"

"Yes."

"Good. You wait in the parlour, I'll fetch her wrap." She went past him, disappeared down a hallway and Mark went back where Eileen was, towered above her. Saw the languid way her face tilted, the dark-rimmed eyes came up almost indifferently and clung to his face.

"Come on, honey, we're going for a little walk."

Mrs. Buell brought her coat, put it around her shoulders and patted her cheek with a broad, strong hand, helped her up and looked past her at Mark.

Outside the old dog lifted his head from the porch-bed he had, sniffed at them and put his head down again, closed his eyes. The night had a filmy drift of high, curved clouds, thin and opaque, overhead. They were bent with the grace of ancient swords, old scimitars. The moon was tilted and glowing in a serenely pale way and the yeasty froth of stars were like minute diamonds, cold and dazzling-clear.

She walked with him. They went east, past other houses and the liquid light touched them, passed them through and plunged them into semi-darkness again. There was a heavy cent of flowers in the gloom, a soft-huddling peacefulness the farther they walked from the main roadway of town.

A gigantic, squat oak, leafed out and casting an enormous shadow hard across a welter of grass, green and furry-soft interspersed with tiny flowers around its rugged base, was limned against the night. He steered her toward it, took her by the shoulders and turned her so that the faint moonlight fell across her face, deepened the shadows that lurked there and was reflected in the solemnity of her eyes, then he dropped his hands and looked at her.

With the night around them, the faintest whispers of sound, of human-kind soft in the distance, the scent of the spring-earth and the solitude, she looked unreal; quiet, granite still and unreal.

Somewhere behind them, down the little roadway where the houses were, a door slammed, a thin voice called to a dog, told him to hurry up and get his dinner before the cat found it. The reedy voice went through both of them, jarred them back to reality. He saw her eyes flicker once, go toward the sound, linger, then come back to a slow contemplation of his face.

He thought of their son, of Carter Diamond, then of the gun with the firing-pin in it, put there by exulting fingers of a little boy whose flushed face, elated fingers, held his treasure in a damp grip.

The voice that had called the dog broke into a peal of laughter and that knifed into them too. Boy-laughter was the same anywhere and in the darkness it could be any boy's voice making it.

She stirred. Looked up at the gnarled branches, past them at the sky, across it to the littlest star, on to the high moon and its fragile loneliness. The line of her throat, the sweep of her jaw, was soft-bracketed by the dull light. The glow of her eyes was bluer, not so dark, the rise and fall of her breast was stronger. The night was working its ancient mystery. What he, nor anyone else, couldn't do, heaven could.

Chapter Seven

He started talking without thoughtfully arranging the words, letting them sound as he felt them. Her gaze came down to his face again and stayed there in dark-liquid inscrutability.

"It goes back a long way, Eileen. Back to Texas when I first knew you. Back to the day we were married and the day when Will was born. I reckon all along we had the difference between us but until I was pretty confirmed in my profession and you had your thoughts about me — and my calling — sorted out, kind of crystallised into the dislike, neither of us ever talked much about these things.

"I expect the first years of any marriage are about like that. Rosy. Pleasant and real wonderful. Then later the differences crop up like ours did. Only I really didn't know how you felt down deep and you didn't make me know. Sure, you pecked at me a little but not enough, I guess, for me to understand. Well, anyway — then you up and left, came

181

here." He looked across at her, saw her eyes on him, her face still, pale in the weak light.

"Then you came here . . . Brought Will with you. I knew then, Eileen. I was knocked into knowing, then, but I didn't understand just how seriously you felt about my being a manhunter before. So — I trailed you, and on the trail I promised myself, and you — and Will — to quit manhunting. To go to stage driving or shoeing or ranching — but so's we could be together. Then *this* happened, Eileen. We lost Will."

"And you went after them — the men who were responsible."

He nodded. "Yes, I went after them, and if it'd been someone else's son I would have gone after them too because men like that can't be left to run loose and kill people like that."

"And you killed them."

He shook his head, gazing at her, seeing the hot moistness of her eyes. "No, I didn't. One I didn't find, exactly. I mean I don't know where he is but I know *who* he is, which means I'll find him all right. I brought the other one in alive. He's in Jonathon Buell's jail right now — alive." He looked appealingly at her. "See, Eileen? I didn't kill him. Nine men out of ten will tell you I had every right to kill him, that I *should* have killed him — but I didn't. Do you understand?"

"Perhaps. Tell me, though, why you didn't."

"Because of you. Because that's the way you feel, the way you think about these things and because maybe you're right. Maybe my kind of law *wasn't* right — the Texas kind. I sort of think maybe it wasn't, myself. Jonathon Buell started me thinking like that. He doesn't run them down; he hardly even goes after them and he gives them every break. Listen, Eileen; I'd pretty well made up my mind about those killers. I was going to wait for one today then kill him when he came up and I had the chance — but I got him to talking and I don't think he killed Will. You see what I mean? A year ago I'd of shot him and called him a liar. Today I brought him back alive. I figured it like Buell would have figured it — like you would have, up to a point, and I brought him back alive."

"Who is he?"

"A man named Erastus Diamond. A mean, dirty dog of a man."

"Was he implicated, when Will was killed?"

"Yes. He told me that, but — "

"I want to see him."

Mark was shocked. "Eileen!"

"I want to see him. Will you take me down where he is?"

"Now? You mean right now?"

"Yes."

He made a despairing motion with one big fist. "You don't want to talk to him, Eileen. He's a mangy brushpopper, not worth listening to."

"I want to talk to him anyway, Mark."

He stood still, staring at her, then his shoulders slumped in resignation. "Yes — if you insist, but it's wrong. It isn't good for you, Eileen. Wait a while at least."

Her lips curved upwards, colour was back in her cheeks. She reached out and touched him. "Mark, you did try, I know you did. I thought — I'd lost you when I came here. Then I found you again when you came and I lost Will — then — I knew you'd gone after them and I thought I'd lost you again, forever that time, because Will wasn't here to bind us together any more."

He caught her hand, held it in his fist. "You couldn't lose me, Eileen. No matter where you went, even if I couldn't find you, you'd never be able to lose me. I'd live in your memory just like you will always live in mine. Like Will lives in both our memories and always will. The things we've made out of our lives never die, Eileen. I've learnt that this last week — less than a week — since I've been here in Cascade. I've learnt a lot of other things, too."

"About being a lawman, Mark?"

"Yes, about being a lawman. I came here knowing enough about being a lawman, the way the law should work."

"And Jonathon Buell taught you differently?"

Mark shook his head. "Not exactly. He *showed* me a lot. Showed me there's got to be a lot of understanding and tolerance in a manhunter."

"No," she said, standing erect, moving off the the tree's trunk. "Not in a manhunter, Mark, in a lawman. A manhunter is what you've always been. That's what frightened me."

He looked puzzled.

"There's a difference, Mark. You've always said there's got to be law and lawmen. I never said you were wrong; what I said was that a manhunter isn't a lawman so much as he's a wolf — a hunting animal who hunts other men because he loves to hunt them. A manhunter's not a lawman, he's a separate breed of men, like a wolf is a separate breed of dog or coyote or fox. I told you a dozen times there wasn't any difference between the manhunter and the men he hunts; that actually I've always thought the manhunter was the worst of the two. He hunts men for their bounty, their reward, or because he loves to grind other men into the earth, to beat them, to kill them. He doesn't do it because he's trying to uphold the law, Mark. That's secondary; that's incidental. He wants to beat them, to kill them to show that he's the best man. Like a wolf, Mark." She took two small steps and was up close to him. Close enough so he could smell the same pine-soap scent he'd smelled in her hair the first day in Cascade.

"I wouldn't stop you from being a lawman, Mark. I never wanted to stop you from that, exactly. It was the other thing I feared. I feared it even more when I saw how Will was idolising you, trying his hardest to be exactly like you. It was too much, Mark." She was staring up into his face, her eyes large and midnight-blue.

"That was the deepest hurt of all, Mark, next to the loss of Will — the deepest hurt of all. You were a manhunter, a professional wolf killing from behind a badge."

"I didn't kill Diamond today," he said.

"I know. I'm grateful. More grateful than you imagine because it means I haven't lost you." She stepped back a little. "Take me down there, Mark, where Diamond is."

His mind was fogged with doubt and struggling understanding. He was essentially an uncomplicated man, even simple in an honest and forthright way. Right then he didn't understand his wife but he tried to. He walked beside her up the dark and rutted roadway toward the central section of Cascade trying to understand a woman's emotionalism and not quite grasping it at all.

Jonathon and Carter were playing checkers when Mark threw open the door. They looked up at the same time and smiled at him, then both faces froze as Eileen came into the little room.

She stopped stock-still.

Carter's scrubbed face and wide eyes made the savage purple slash down across his face stand out in dark prominence. His tousled head caught and held the lamp-light. Jonathon got up and the boy followed his example, instinctively.

Mark moved past them, turned and threw a look at his wife's face. His heart was thudding sturdily, loudly, in its hidden darkness. "She wants to see Ras Diamond, Jonathon."

The constable's jaw sagged. "Ras?" He smiled in a sickly way. "Naw, Eileen, you don't want to see that scoundrel."

She went closer to Carter and Jonathon whipped from behind his desk and pulled up his chair for her. She sat in it, lifted a hand and traced out the livid bruise with a cool finger. "Did you fall?" she asked.

Cart was red to the roots of his corn-husk hair at her touch. "No'm. Got hit in the face with a quirt."

Her hand jerked away, fell into her lap. She looked up at Mark then around to Jonathon then back to Carter again. "Who hit you?"

"My pa — Mister Diamond."

She leaned back in the chair and Carter folded and unfolded his hands in his lap. Looking at Mark she said, "The same man?"

He nodded. "Yes. This is Carter, Eileen. That's his first name. Carter, this is Miz' Carter — uh — that's her *last* name."

Carter smiled, flushed a deeper red and locked his hands together in an agonised knot.

No one spoke while she gazed at the boy, at his thinness, his large blue eyes, his wealth of unruly hair, his smallness contrasted against those in the room with him — and the brutal mark across his face.

She finally looked around at Jonathon. "Can I see Mister Diamond?"

Jonathon's eyes flicked to Mark and back again. "Ma'm," he said slowly, "Are you plumb sure you want to. Y'know, he was one of the men who stoled the horses your

188

boy was guarding."

"Yes," she said, "I know. Can I see him?"

Jonathon bobbed his head, looked across at Mark. "You take her in. Cart and I'll wait out here."

Mark scooped up the horseshoe key-ring and moved toward the cell-room door without a word. Eileen arose and followed him. Carter looked after them a moment then turned back to the checker-board. He had to speak to draw Jonathon's attention away from the door across the room which Mark had closed behind himself and his wife.

"She's sure pretty, Mister Buell, isn't she?"

Jonathon's head lowered a little. He studied Cart's face, then, without answering moved a man on the checkerboard.

Mark had never been in the cell-room before but there wasn't much to it, four steel-strap cages bolted to the north wall of the building, light, such as there was, came from two lamps hanging overhead one at each end of the room. Daylight had access through three long slits, almost like ports, or rifle-slits, cut into the wall several feet above the tops of the cells. Beyond the steel strips were men. Mark peered closely. The first one was an obvious drunk, the second was Ras Diamond and the third was a tall, gawkingly thin man stooped at the shoulders in his effort to see Eileen in the murky light. Mark ignored the last man, walked over to the door of Diamond's cage and unlocked it, motioned with his hand for Diamond to come out. He came, slitted eyes furtive and hating. Mark took him by the arm and started toward the door with him.

Eileen said, "No, Mark. Up there."

Mark stopped and looked. At the westernmost end of the long narrow cell-room was a distant corner. He hustled Diamond toward it and Eileen followed. Beyond earshot of the other felons, Mark swung the prisoner around. Eileen was standing between Diamond and the peering faces far down the room. She said nothing. Diamond squirmed, waited a while then looked up at Mark.

"What th' devil's this about? She got something t'say to me?"

A hard thumb went into his ribs, a harder voice, low, said, "Shut up!"

Diamond jerked from the thumb, made a grimace of pain and looked at Eileen again. He was uncomfortable under her unblinking regard. Then she spoke.

"Did you know that little boy who was killed? I'm his mother."

Diamond's face contorted. "Lady, I didn't kill him. I didn't see no shot fired by anyone."

"But you heard one," Mark said.

"I think I heard two, yes, but lady. I didn't fire at *no* one. No kid — no one — and that's gospel truth."

She fell silent again. The staring continued. Ras squirmed but endured it. Finally she said, "You have a little boy, too, haven't you? Isn't that your son in the office?"

"In the office?" Ras said swiftly. "I got no kid in the office nor anywhere else. I don't *want* no kid. I don't want one near me. Does that answer you, lady?"

Eileen looked puzzled. At that second Jonathon Buell stepped into the cell-room and squinted up at them. "Just wondered," he said. "Couldn't hear anything and just wondered how you were making out."

Mark's dark eyes, black in the shadows, were imploring. He said, "Come on, honey. You've seen the weasel, now let's go."

She might have hesitated, have answered negatively, but Ras Diamond was of a mind with Mark. He edged closer to the big Texan and mumbled to him.

"Take me back. She gives me the creeps."

Mark took him back, locked him in and saw the tall, thin man in the next stall staring at him. He ignored it, turned his back on them both and went back to Eileen, took her arm and guided her out into Jonathon's office. Carter twisted around, half smiling at them. Jonathon sighed mightily and stood up.

"Would you sort of mind things for me for a while now, Mark. I'm hungrier'n a bear."

Mark nodded. Jonathon put on his hat, winked swiftly at Carter, made a funny little bow to Eileen and left.

Left alone the three of them sat in awkward silence. Carter had two checkers in his hands. He kept pressing one against the other one, looking down to do it as though the affair was one of great delicacy and importance. Eileen watched him for a long time. Mark finally twisted up a cigarette, lit it and dropped down into Jonathon's old chair, lay his hat on the desk and looked at its dusty, graceful, curling edges.

"Why did you want to see him, Eileen?"

"To satisfy myself," she said. "I can't believe there's a man living who would deliberately shoot a little boy. I still don't believe it."

Mark looked at his cigarette. "Not him. He didn't do it. I don't believe that either."

Her gaze swept up to his face, to the copper-hued light reflected off his hair from the lamp's dull glow, then her head turned a little and she was looking at Carter again, seeing the unruly hair, the painfully clean, stiffly new and ill-fitting clothes, the boots with their toe-plates, the downcast head and the working small hands.

"Isn't Mister Diamond your father, son?"

Cart looked up, shot Mark an appealing glance then looked her straight in the eyes. "No'm. My real father's dead. My real mother too." His mouth stayed open, shaping words, but no more came and he let his gaze wander to Mark again.

The awkward silence hung, torturing each of them, until Jonathon returned then Mark stood up. Carter's eyes flashed from one adult face to the other. Lingered longest on Mark's. Jonathon smoothed the shirt over his stomach self-consciously, groping for something to say. Mark moved around the desk, stopped at Eileen's side and looked down at her. As though responding to his thoughts she turned toward the door. He held it open for her, waiting. Halfway through she turned and looked at Carter again, then disappeared outside and Mark followed her, closed the door and left the old constable and the be-wildered youngster staring at it.

Jonathon sat down, inched forward to the edge of his chair, folded his fingers together and said, "Now, Cart — tell me exactly what they said while I was gone."

Carter told him. Crinkled up his forehead to remember and told him all of it.

Jonathon studied the boy's face a moment in silence, then leaned back in his chair — and smiled.

Mark walked slowly down the little side-street with her. He didn't offer anything but his company. Apparently that was enough because she didn't hurry; made no effort to end the evening until they were at the picket gate with the old dog snuffling through it at them in a garrulous way. Then she faced him. Raised one hand and touched his cheek with it.

"I know, Mark."

He was perplexed so wisely kept still.

"You bought him those boots, the new shirt and trousers, didn't you?"

"Yes'm."

"Did you find him up in the hills?"

"Well, in a way, yes. He was running away. I trailed him and brought him back."

She nodded softly. "A lost little boy and a man who was lost, too. Is he why you didn't kill Diamond, Mark?"

"No. I told you why I didn't kill Diamond. Because I believed him when he said he had no hand in what happened to Will. And because — the law's different here."

"Good night, Mark." She opened the gate,

194

entered and closed it behind her. The old dog whined and snuffled at her feet.

"Eileen?"

She turned, stood close to the gate looking at him.

"Eileen — we're still —," he couldn't find the word and said, "folks — aren't we?"

"Yes, Mark. We're still folks. We always were; we always will be. Mark? What are you going to do with him?"

"With Carter? Get him a room at the hotel. Maybe we can fix him up a bed at your house down the road, later, if you want to."

"I want to," she said very softly. "Good night, Mark."

"Eileen? I'll be here in the morning."

"I know you will. Good night, Mark."

He went back uptown, through the dwindling noise and past the saloons, across the road to the constable's office and entered. Jonathon and Carter were laughing about something. They bit it off sharp when he entered, looked up at him, waiting. He sat down and felt for his tobacco sack, lowered his head to make the cigarette and spoke like that, head down, occupied.

"Jonathon, if you'll bed Carter down in my diggings at the hotel I'll run down something that's on my mind."

Jonathon sat like stone, watching the cigarette curl up into shape, then he got up heavily. "Something I'd like you to see first, Mark, if you got a minute." He looked down at Carter. "We can bed Cart down on the way."

Mark looked up quizzically but Jonathon was already reaching for his hat. Mark got up with a shrug, smiled at Carter and followed Jonathon outside. They crossed the road with the boy between them, found the dark doorway and the narrow stairs that led up to Mark's room, went up and Mark let Carter into the room.

"Bed down, Cart. We'll see you in the morning. Anything you want?"

"No," the boy said, eyeing the bed, the booted carbine in a corner, the worn saddlebags dangling from an iron clothes rack. "I'll see you in the morning."

"Good night, son," Jonathon said.

"Good night, Mister Buell."

Mark put out his big hand and the boy took it, his fist lost in the larger one. "We worked like pardners together, Cart," he said. "We'll make out."

The boy swallowed and nodded and didn't open his mouth.

Jonathon led the way back downstairs. He turned north and stumped up the walk with Mark beside him. At the doctor's house he slid into an alley behind the home and stopped where a small shed was locked, set off a way from the residence. Mumbling in the gloom he fumbled for the right key, swung the door inward and motioned Mark ahead. Inside it was as dark as the inside of a well. Jonathon struck two matches before he got the lamp going, then he walked around Mark to a long table, reached down and pulled back the grey canvas. The grisly remains of a man lay there exposed.

"That's the feller got killed last night, Mark. Take a good look and tell me what you think."

Mark went closer, stared down at the body in a long moment of silence. There was dried blood on the corpse, but low, down around his belt, on his pants-legs, over his boots. His head an awry look but no skin was broken. The man's skull had apparently been crushed without breaking the skin. He probably hadn't died from the blow for several minutes after he'd received it. Mark bent from the waist and studied the face. It was totally unknown to him. He straightened up, turned away. Jonathon flicked the canvas back into place and led the way back outside, locked the door and walked slowly down the alley to the roadway and headed back uptown. Mark walked beside him in silence.

"Well; what do you think, boy?"

"Like you say, Jonathon, he got clouted on the side of the head. Maybe the killer jumped out at him and he heard him or something; anyway he apparently turned just before the club got him. Maybe some of the blow was taken in the body — the shoulder maybe — enough of the slam taken out so it didn't knock him out."

"Oh," Jonathon said knowingly, "he wasn't knocked out. It's one of those strange things that happen. You or me'd have gone down like a pole-axed steer. This feller had a skull of iron, it looks like."

Mark shrugged. "I wasn't thinking about that, specially, Jonathon. I was thinking about the blood."

Jonathon stopped and looked up at Mark. "What about the blood?" he asked, not moving, still gazing intently at the larger, younger man.

"It isn't his," Mark said.

Jonathon's mouth lifted in a thin smile. "You're sure, are you?"

Mark looked at him, scowling. "His skull got cracked but his hide wasn't broken, Jonathon. Where did the blood come from then, unless he's got a bullethole under his clothes."

"No," Jonathon said with a wag of his

head, the little smile lingering, "he's got no hole in him anywhere."

"Then the blood — say, Jonathon — didn't you tell me this feller put up a scrap before he cashed in?"

"I did. I also told you he had a Bowie knife. I found it right near his fist when the doc and I went up there in doc's wagon to get his carcass. The knife's over at the — "

"Then that would account for the blood, Jonathon. It isn't his — you know that. He must have gotten in a swipe at his attacker with that Bowie."

Jonathon resumed his walking, Mark caught up with him but he was looking straight ahead, his mouth drawn inward with concentration. They wound their way through the late pedestrians, through the light that straggled across the plankwalk and lay in puddles in the road, down off the plankwalk and into the roadway, across it toward the constable's office and just as they were stepping up on the far side, Mark spoke.

"I think I know who killed him, Jonathon."

Jonathon didn't turn or slow his stride or speak until he had opened the office door and marched inside, then he turned while reaching up to thumb back his hat and said, "Who?"

"Ras Diamond."

"Why? What makes you think so?"

Mark slouched, staring at Jonathon. "Get him out here. Let's see if I'm right."

"Sure." Jonathon went into the cell-room and came back out with a puffy-eyed Erastus Diamond. The prisoner's small eyes flashed to Mark in an indignant, rebellious way.

"Now what the hell?"

Mark nodded his head. "Take off your shirt, Diamond."

"What?" The little eyes widened.

"Take off your shirt!"

Diamond looked at the constable uncertainly then back to Mark. He shrugged and began to loosen the buttons. With a final shrug he removed the garment.

Mark and Jonathon stood in silence, looking at him. There was a rough bandage across his chest, held in place by several turns over his left shoulder.

"Bird kick you?" Mark said softly, derisively.

"I fell on some rocks when I was out lookin' f'cattle."

"That's a lie," Mark said. "Do you want me to tell you how you got that gash?"

"Go ahead."

"You got it from a Bowie knife. Want to know how *I* know; because I was around in back of your cabin last night when your missus was bandaging the thing. You cussed like a mule-skinner, Diamond. You talked about how you got it and you cussed about Cart running off." He was bluffing about some of what he'd heard but he was gambling that the rest of it would strike home. It did.

Diamond's face blanched, his eyes narrowed and the ripple along his cheek showed where he had clamped his jaws tightly closed.

Jonathon picked up the shirt, held it out. "Put it back on, Ras." He watched the prisoner shrug back into the shirt. "Where'd you hide the money?"

"I didn't do it."

Mark caught him by the shirt front like he'd done earlier, almost lifted him off his feet, swept him up close. "If you say you didn't do it, Diamond, the law's going to turn you out of here. If you're a free man, out there in the roadway, I'll be a free man too because I'm no longer a lawman. If we're both free I'm going to call you, Diamond. Call you where the whole damned town can see you get beat to the draw. Gut-shoot you, Diamond." He took his hand away and Erastus Diamond stumbled, put one hand over his mouth and wiped it crossways as though to brush away the terror that was in him, deep down.

Mark turned to Jonathon. "He didn't do it, constable. You got no right to hold him. We can't prove he did it. Turn him out."

Jonathon was unruffled. His gaze hung to Mark's face a moment then he went around him to Ras Diamond, shot the frightened outlaw a scornful look, crossed to his desk, took a gun out of a drawer, checked it for load, went back beside Diamond and dropped the weapon, carelessly, loosely, in the flapping holster at Diamond's hip. "Sure," he said. "I'll be glad to turn him out. Go on, Ras, like this feller says, I can't hold you without proof. Go on — get out."

Diamond shook his head vigorously. "No," he said. "I'm not going out. You got t'protect me, Jonathon." Mark started toward him. Diamond sidled away.

"I'll *throw* you out," Mark said. His hand went up, reaching, when Diamond bleated to Jonathon.

"I killed him. I killed him with a club, Jonathon. I — you can't turn me loose now."

Mark stopped, his hand fell to his side like a big maul, the clenched fist opened, hung limply. The fire went out of his eyes and he turned toward Jonathon, shrugged and stepped from between the two men. Jonathon's face didn't alter expression. He took the gun from Diamond's holster and tossed it on his desk. "Tell us about it, Erastus, or shall we tell you?"

"I was waitin' f'Darrel Timmons. He said he'd be back last night. He had to fetch his stuff from his shack, then he and me was going on. Goin' west. He'd been in trouble at Bordenton, figured the law over there suspicioned him. I was waitin' for him close by the trace when along comes this feller. I thought it was Darrel. I walked out of the brush an' flagged him down. It wasn't Darrel, it was this messenger. He asked me was I in trouble, bein' afoot an' all, and I figured he had something — was carryin' something — worthwhile, so I says yes, my horse's trapped under a tree limb that fell on us and it's too big f'one man to lift. He gets down and goes back into the trees with me . . ."

"You picked up a club and brained him."

"Yeah. On'y he didn't fall down. He run, of all the damned fool things. He run back t'the road where his horse was. I chased him with the club. He got to staggerin' pretty bad an' I jumped him again. This time he come around so quick I missed with my club an' like to falled. The scut had a Bowie knife an' before I could get my balance he'd slashed me. I rolled away, got up and run at him again. We was mincin' aroun', him

203

gettin' wobblier an' me lookin' for a chance to hit him another lick, when he just falls down. I went over t'see an' he was as dead as a shot horse."

"So," Mark said, "you robbed him. How much longer did you wait for Timmons?"

"I didn't. I went home because I was runnin' blood."

"Your wife patched you up, I know. I heard that through the wall. Where's the messenger's money; what did he have with him?"

"Some bank letters — no money in 'em. I burnt 'em. His money — he only had a hundred dollars. I took that — I hid it at my cabin."

"Along with the rest of your loot," Mark said.

"No, gospel truth," Diamond protested. "Darrel's got the loot from the robberies."

Mark looked at Jonathon, the constable jerked his head at Diamond, took him back into the cell-room and locked him up, returned to the office grimly smiling.

"That was good, Mark. Real good."

Mark made a wry headshake. "No it wasn't. You see, Jonathon, when I first caught him he told me he was a sick man. I remembered what he said when I eavesdropped last night. He didn't say anything about robbing the courier but he said plenty about the way his wife was bandaging him. I thought of those things when we were wondering whose blood was on that feller in the doctor's shack. I knew Diamond was a no-good and a stage robber. The killing didn't happen very far from his turn-off, from what you'd said. It all just seemed to fit together."

Jonathon glanced at his big pocket watch then up at Mark's face. "All right, Mark. You solved that murder for me real neat, now I want you to take a ride with me out a ways."

Mark looked inquisitively curious. "Right now — tonight?"

"Yeh. It's important. Important to you and Eileen, Mark, and to your boy."

"Let's go."

They rode north out of Cascade and just when Mark thought they might be going up the road to the country by Gunsight Notch or the Diamond ranch, Jonathon reined west. Then something stirred in Mark. He paced his friend without speaking, his spirit dropping lower and lower as they rode toward a spot he would never forget as long as he lived.

The night was hushed around them, beams of late moonlight fell in tumbled disarray around the outcroppings, the brush patches and the declivities, shallow and lilting, that coursed the range.

"There," Jonathon said and got down off his horse, fished in his pockets as he led his animal closer, toward a great dark shape, rounded, asprawl, in the near distance. "Give me a match, Mark." Mark handed him several, dismounting as he did so, grim visaged, tight looking up around the eyes. He trailed after Jonathon until they were standing close to the dead horse. Mark's insides were fisted in a hard knot that pained him.

Jonathon leaned forward, peered closer and struck a match, held it low so that he could see the animal closely. The flickering light danced across his face, made it look like it was twisted into a bitter grimace.

"Look here, Mark."

Mark went closer, his eyes mirroring the pain clearly. He bent when Jonathon struck the second match.

"See where that horse got it, Mark? Right in the poll. See those powder burns?" The match went out. Jonathon straightened up looking at the younger man, waiting.

Mark came up slower, his eyes pin-pointed, his mouth bloodless. He turned to his horse, toed into the stirrup and said, "Anything else?"

"No."

He mounted and wheeled his horse. Jonathon clambered aboard and rode slowly after him. He didn't come up until they were back at the stage road, then both swung southward, riding stirrup to stirrup, and Jonathon finally broke the thick silence.

"That's what I meant a couple days ago, Mark, when I said finding Timmons wasn't what was bothering me. I didn't want an innocent man killed nor a blind one to kill him. Did you understand what you saw back there?"

"Yes."

"The bullet that killed your boy's horse didn't come from *either* Timmons or Diamond, it came from the boy's gun, itself. There's no other way for those powder burns to be there. The hair's plumb scorched away."

They went back to town wrapped in gloom, parted at the liverybarn where Mark stabled his horse and walked through the cool darkness to Jonathon's office. The older man was just entering when Mark got there. He closed the door behind Mark and went to his chair, sank down bone-weary and dry-eyed, waiting. It was a long wait. Mark sat like a stone, looking at the floor for endless minutes before he spoke.

"I — didn't look, Jonathon; was there powder burn around the wound in — him — too?"

"Yes."

"I see," Mark said dully. "Something happened. Maybe Timmons and Diamond shot at him, maybe they didn't, whether they did or not they missed him. The horse bolted . . ." He looked up at Jonathon. "I didn't even check his gun."

"I wouldn't have either, Mark, if it'd been my boy."

"Had it been fired?"

"Four times, Mark."

"Four times. He shot at them when they came in fast and stampeded the horses. Maybe that's what made his own horse run away with him." The dark eyes were unblinkingly regarding the older man. "What's the rest of it, Jonathon?"

"You're right up to now. The horse fell, Mark. His right foreleg's broke at the pastern. He fell. Fell on Will. He was threshing around, hurting the boy. Will shot him; put the gun right up against his poll and shot him so's he quit threshing around." Jonathon stopped, licked his lips and looked at the ceiling, the wall, then back at Mark again. "This is the hardest part, Mark. Will's leg was broke under the horse. His back was broke too. He wouldn't have known

208

that. All he knew was that he couldn't stand it . . ."

"He shot himself," Mark said.

"Yes." Jonathon looked down at the jumbled condition of his desk. Papers lay atop papers, handbills, pictures of faces, big black letters offering rewards for men. "But before that he tried to fight off the horse-thieves. He was tryin' to do exactly what he knew his paw would have done. The rest of it wasn't his fault — that horse falling on him, rolling, pinning him under it, but again, he did what a lot of other men, a lot more seasoned men have done under the same circumstances. He did well, Mark, and he died well. You and Eileen can be right proud of him. For a little shaver he was all man."

The silence settled between them again, drew out until it was almost unbearable for Jonathon Buell, then Mark spoke huskily, the words as dry as old cotton.

"I came close to doing what every lawman worth his salt fears he might do someday. I came close to killing a man who wasn't guilty of what I'd already condemned him in my mind for doing."

"No," Jonathon said, "you never were very close, Mark. Not really."

The dark eyes moved like trapped things then Mark reached automatically for his tobacco sack and bent over, his fingers not quite steady, worrying up a cigarette he felt no desire for.

"If I'd found Timmons I'd have killed him, Jonathon."

"Maybe. I doubt that you would have. Anyway, you didn't kill Diamond."

"I was going to. I planned on it, Jonathon. I figured to do it right up until I found Cart back there in the hills. After that . . ."

"Sure; the boy was there. You couldn't kill Diamond in front of him. The lad kept you from it."

"Partly," Mark said. "Partly, I wanted to talk to you first. I didn't know what to do, really. I — I've sort of changed the way I look at things, I guess, but I'll find Timmons. I won't kill him unless he makes me do it, but I think I'd have killed him all right if I'd run across him over at Bordenton."

"That," Jonathon said, "was the one thing that had me scairt worst of all. After you came back from there I wasn't the least bit worried."

The unlit cigarette dangled from Mark's mouth. "You didn't think I'd find him? I've never lost a man yet that I hunted, Jonathon."

"Timmons is the first one you lost then because after Bordenton you never had a chance to find him — never even came close but once, to finding him."

"Do you know where he is?"

"Yes."

"Where?"

"He's in the cell right alongside of Ras Diamond, Mark. That's where he's been since he poked his beak back into Cascade yesterday after he came down from visiting with Ras, so you see, boy, you never had a chance of killing him." Jonathon leaned forward. "Mark — if you'd killed him — think of Eileen . . ."

"Yes, I have thought of that. I've thought of that ever since I got my senses back, but at first, right after we found — "

"I know. That was when I worried the most. I expect any man would react the same way; me too, if I'd had a thing like that happen to me, only I could see what you were trying so cussed hard to do and I knew it was all wrong, Mark. It wouldn't help, it would ruin everything from here on." Jonathon paused, inspected his palms then went on.

"Mark; I've seen a lot of good men turned bad by some things like that. Seen 'em do things I *knew* they were going to ruin themselves by doing. After a quarter century of seeing things like that, well, you get to the place where you interfere like I interfered in your case. It wasn't any of my business, but I didn't want this thing to go sour on you, make you another killer wandering around like a half-crazy wolf, killing to stay alive, killing for revenge, killing until you got killed, and believe me, Mark, that's how it goes. By God I know!"

Mark lit the cigarette, inhaled a big gust of smoke, held it a moment then let it trickle out his nose and mouth. "I'm grateful to you, Jonathon. I'm not very good with words — I found that out again today — but if I knew the right ones to say to you I'd say 'em."

Jonathon took up his old hat, slapped fine dust out of its floppy hatbrim and spoke while he worked. "There's nothing to say, Mark. I got more'n I could have expected out of this. I got a friend — three friends, really — you an' Eileen and Carter — and I had another friend. I reckon we'll remember him, Mark, a long, long time. But I'm humbly grateful for a couple of things, too. Grateful Cart's finally found someone who'll steer him, sort of, give him chances and be around to back up his play when he needs it later on in life. I'm grateful you came up out of Texas, 'cause I'm damned sick and tired of this job. I want to spend the next sixty years fishin' and pokin' around in the back country. I spent the last sixty years forkin' horses and trying to out-guess renegades. It's interesting, Mark, but it gets old too, like me." Jonathon stood up and tried a smile. "I've done more damned talking this last half hour than I've done in ten years and now I'm hungry. Why don't you come home with me, boy. We'll have some supper and maybe Eileen'll sit on the porch with you for a spell."

"The funeral's at eight," Mark said, arising.

"I'm not likely to forget," Jonathon said, opening the door, waiting until Mark was through it to blow down the lamp chimney and swear mildly at the lock on the door, which eluded him, then fought against being snapped closed.

They walked through the darkness with the diminishing sounds of Cascade's night-life around them. Went through the humped-up ruts of the road Jonathon's house was on with the richly splashed Universe up there as cooly aloof as it always was and Mark sought the littlest star, the faint, sad beauty of the lean moon, the strange, benign magic of the night that went down into a man and winnowed out his bitterness, his suffering.

"Tomorrow we say good-bye to Will," he said aloud.

The constable's lumpy figure plodded along, head down, arms swinging. "No one can ever take that burden from you and Eileen, boy, but remember that tomorrow is also something else. It's the start of a new life and the only people who don't deserve much of life, Mark, are those who don't profit from their hurts. Remember that."

"I will," Mark said, looking closely at Jonathon Buell. "You're the darndest lawman I ever knew. I've told you that before, haven't I? I don't mean the darndest exactly, Jonathon. Like I said, I'm a poor man with words. I mean the greatest. If I hadn't come out of Texas after Eileen, I reckon I never would have thought of lawing as anything more than manhunting."

"Well," Jonathon said as they turned in at the gate, the old dog whimpering ecstatically around Jonathon's bowed legs. "Well, then I reckon the Lord's taken something away, Mark, but I reckon he's also give something too."

They went up to the house, and in . . .

Lauran Paine who, under his own name and various pseudonyms has written over 900 books, was born in Duluth, Minnesota, a descendant of the Revolutionary War patriot and author, Thomas Paine. His family moved to California when he was at an early age and his apprenticeship as a Western writer came about through the years he spent in the livestock trade, rodeos, and even motion pictures where he served as an extra because of his expert horsemanship in several films starring movie cowboy Johnny Mack Brown. In the late 1930s, Paine trapped wild horses in northern Arizona and even, for a time, worked as a professional farrier. Paine came to know the Old West through the eyes of many who had been born in the previous century and he learned that Western life had been very different from the way it was portrayed on the screen. "I knew men who had killed other men," he later recalled. "But they were the exceptions. Prior to and during the Depression, people were just too busy eking out an existence to indulge in Saturday-night brawls." He served in the U.S. Navy in the Second World War and began writing for Western pulp magazines following his discharge. It is interesting to note that all of his earliest novels (written under his own name and the pseudonym Mark Carrel) were published in the British market and he soon had as strong a following in that country as in the United States. Paine's Western fiction is characterized by strong plots, authenticity, an apparently effortless ability to construct situation and character, and a preference for building his stories upon a solid foundation of historical fact. ADOBE EMPIRE (1956), one of his best novels, is a fictionalized account of the last twenty years in the life of trader William Bent and, in an off-trail way, has a melancholy, bittersweet texture that is not easily forgotten. MOON PRAIRIE (1950), first published in the United States in 1994, is a memorable story set during the mountain man period of the frontier. In later novels such as THE HOMESTEADERS (1986) or THE OPEN RANGE MEN (1990), he showed that the special magic and power of his stories and characters had only matured along with his basic themes of changing times, changing attitudes, learning from experience, respecting nature, and the yearning for a simpler, more moderate way of life.

DISCARD